A
SWORD
GIRL
NOVEL
•

LA MAUPIN

Jordan Stratford

Published by Outland Entertainment LLC
3119 Gillham Road
Kansas City, MO 64109

Founder/Creative Director: Jeremy D. Mohler
Editor-in-Chief: Alana Joli Abbott

ISBN: 978-1-954255-27-2 (Print),
ISBN: 978-1-954255-28-9 (eBook)
Worldwide Rights
Created in the United States of America

Developmental Editor: Zig Zag Claybourne
Copy Editor: Bessie Mazur
Cover Illustration: Chris Yarbrough
Cover Design: Jeremy D. Mohler
Interior Layout: Mikael Brodu

Visit **outlandentertainment.com** to see more,
or follow us on our Facebook Page
facebook.com/outlandentertainment/

I

From a letter found in the Biblioteque Nationale
attributed to Mme. Julie La Maupin.
1688—la Bastille

There is fever, which weaves thought and fear together into a tangle of words. It comes from the chill of the walls. Perhaps there are too many prayers for death in such a place, so fever lurks, awaiting invitation. It is not much, just an uncomfortable heat on my forehead, and a thirst, though the water here is at least fit enough. I am hungry. But there is paper, and ink, while I wait for bread. Should my jailers remember, or care.

Like the hours at Avignon, in the convent of the Visitandines, the candle makes the hours go, and prayer blurs the walls of my prison. There are faces in the shadows, as memory paints them: Sérannes, and the shape of his mouth, and when in recollection I taste his skin there is the salt of the sea, and Marseilles. Lisette, and the line from her throat to her collarbone that caused an ache in me, and the flame becomes the glow of the convent fire roaring so loud it shook the earth beneath our horses, heat behind us and before us only the night sky and the thin road, a pilgrims road, and then in Paris in the Café Procope and the steam of coffee sweetened with pink sugar and poor Lully is dead, masterful Lully is dead and I am seventeen and we all the actors of the city have come to mourn him, over coffee. And d'Albert, sweet d'Albert who called me Emilie when he kissed me. Somewhere now in a cell like this one, for the same crime, and in this at least we are together. And elsewhere, my husband. My poor husband and his boundless kindness. Shamed to think of him now at last.

It is the fever or the sleeplessness that jumbles my words so. A marvel that my fingers can keep up.

There is more paper here, so I need not write crosswise over the page, and I will continue until sleep takes me or the guards rattle me to fear and to whatever fate awaits me now.

The price for what I have done is death. Not my first crime, nor my first death sentence, should it come to it.

I am a murderess. Ten men, they say, although it was only six by my hand and barely that, more from their wounds and ill care. Drunkards all and dead only for their lack of sous to call anyone with the common sense of a midwife or a stablehand—any seamstress could have saved them, but wine thins the blood. And therein is the whole story writ out.

I am a seductress, and in the circles into which I was born this too is punishable by death, by pox or birthing-bed or exile. I am the breaker of sacred vows, both to my husband and to God, although it was God who cut my hair and this I have yet to forgive. I am a thief, when I have had to have been— as an actress, one rarely gets to choose the role in which one is cast.

They think prison will break me, but they forget I have been a nun. Cold walls and thin gruel and hours of solitude; these are things I have sought out, games I have played and pieces I have moved in the pursuit of love. Every step a performance, every face a mask, every lover a character. In this last scene I wore my best dress, danced to perfection, kissed a girl, insulted a fool, dueled with pretty boys and taught a lesson in blood and muscle and steel. And so, the scene changes, and there is the luffing of the candle, the scratch of paper, and the chill from stone walls.

I do not know how this play will end.

God, for a sword in my hand at this moment.

For a sword in my hand.

1686 —Two years earlier

My fingers are sticky with blood.

It is a simple mistake, *his* simple mistake in taking the measure, but his sword pushes a cut into my chest, below the collar bone, above the heart. There is no pain, not yet—and the look on his face, the poor boy! He freezes, and I smile.

I know precisely how to punish him.

I lay my point across the top of his thigh and turn my wrist, drawing the point in an arc across his flesh the full width of my palm. Just a scratch, really, or more than that, but ever slightly, and it is what I want. His touch an accident, mine deliberate. Knowing this makes me feel bigger than I ever have before.

And there is not too much blood, just enough.

I know now that I can have anything I bleed for. Anything I show up for. And a little blood will wash away with salt, when I'm ready. I'll gift the blouse to the maid's daughter, when she mends it.

I hope it leaves a scar. A little pink line to remind me to keep my guard up. I pray that it is the right sort of pink. Rather exactly.

I think about colours a great deal. It seems everywhere they are pushed into other colours they do not wish to be. Harder. I lament that every dress has to look like a jewel—dark and deep and like a stone. I'm sure there are proper words for colours, but I do not know them. Pale colours are for the poor, the girls here say, and you can tell. The families that can afford the dyers so they too can look like jewels, but the girls from the lieutenants' families, the colours are ever so softer. Watered-down. I prefer them, though I know I'm not to.

They all—we all, I suppose—are meant to look like the shiniest apples on the cart. While my friends and their sisters and even their maid's sisters all seem to struggle with it, it is the simplest thing in the world for me, so much so that I find it dull. A raise of a shoulder, a look and a look away. Then there are little gifts and little compliments and a nod to my father, but when I roll my eyes or even laugh, he is cross with me. I'm to take this seriously, me in a dress too orange or too blue for my liking.

Not that I am any kind of flower myself. I can groom a horse as well as any of my father's men, and ride well, and throw a rock as far as any boy— although there is one farm boy who can make a tree crack at fifty paces, and I wish I could do that.

But *this* boy, this bleeding boy before me catching his breath and mortified by the fact that we are both bleeding—what did he expect from this? This line of sawdust, with the forest behind us, and a barn to shield us from gossiping eyes, swords levelled at one another. God knows where his came from, and what filth its point has been dragged through. I shall wash the wound thoroughly when I return home, this lasting gift from the clumsy boy.

He showed me his thing behind the stables once, years ago, and I laughed so hard he threatened to pee on me. He is an idiot. I told Elise and she said the same thing happened to her, so the next day I let him kiss me. But he was shy, like a cousin. I'm not even sure I know his name.

But we have written little names in each other's flesh, and that is something.

———◄●►———

My horse is called Lilas.

Father trains me with the grooms. Not every day, but sometimes. I can clean a saddle and pick a hoof, and I must groom Lilas myself every time before I go riding.

After grooming we ride. I am not allowed to ride bareback anymore, as I did when I was very little, but now must ride sidesaddle. Mine has a horn over which I can hook my knee, so it is not so bad, but much more difficult than riding astride as the grooms do. I am a good rider, tall and straight, and neither afraid of the whip nor cruel with it.

Mostly it is a chance for me to be alone, Lilas and I. Alone enough, though always in company and never too far out of sight. We always ride south, into the sun, into the warmth, and to the stand of pines, which mark the end of royal grounds. Past the carts of stone, the parade of tradesmen and cloth merchants, the ice-carts of butchers and fishmongers, so many men and horses constantly flowing into the palace, and only Lilas and me flowing away from it, away from the shining, golden stink of it. Toward the pines.

———◆———

I have read these books of letters, which are popular at Court, and realize I have begun my story not at all properly. I have yet to come up with something truly scandalous, but with all the bum-grabbing around here and not much to do but gossip, I am certain to think of something.

My name is Julie Emilie d'Aubigny. My father is Gaston d'Aubigny, Secretary to Louis de Lorraine-Guise, Count of Armagnac and Master of Horse to the King, Louis XIV. It is the forty-third year of his reign. I am sixteen years of age.

My mother clucks to her maid, my father to his mistress, my brothers grown, or dead, and I am left much to my own amusement after Mass each morning. In the afternoons I am tutored with the pages here, and study writing and grammar with the other palace daughters, and drawing. In music I love to sing—in Italian although it displeases my tutor. It is fashionable to sing only the new operas in French, but I find the Italian lighter, and prettier, so I collect these songs in my head and sing them only when alone. In dance I am tutored privately, and sometimes I dance with the other court girls. But all of this after Mass.

Mass is a kind of price paid by all those born to money, and in the orbit of Court. Attendance ensures how one's value is perceived—I have said "the shiniest apple on the cart" and yes, we girls all in a row, veiled and silent, heads bowed, the price of the apples remains high. I have seen how it grates the other girls, some of whom are my friends, clever and pretty. They are dragged to it and flee from it. But I adore it, the theatre of it, the beauty of the music and deliberation of each movement. Everything including the washing of the performer's hands is done with care, with presence. It is probably blasphemy to think so. So, for me it is all a play, and a beautiful one, and when it is my part, I too, have steps and lines to recite.

The chairs are uncomfortable, but so are shoes, and the trick is to remain as upright as a tulip. Even sitting is dancing. Tall spine, shoulders down, chin high when unbowed, head back, hands either clasped and motionless, or, to evoke perfect piety, palms open softly on the lap.

The worst is all the brown. The oppressive brown of the wood, in the panels, on the floor, of the furniture. Brown, brown, brown. Even gold in a girls' chapel seems to be some drab metal, dragging brown into an attention with which it is not comfortable.

The boys at the altar tend to be friends' younger brothers, the second brother for most families, bound for the cloth. I see how they giggle and fidget and fart or fumble as they hand the priest something. But some move with grace and I think there, there is a dancer. And the singing is always beautiful—but the King has declared it thus; everything here is to be beautiful.

I say this knowing full well the life of horses, and their sweat and their rutting and their shit. But this is shoveled away hourly, just as I've seen filth in the halls of the Palace, and the hasty attendance of servants to remove dropped food or puddles of piss from otherwise immaculate marble. That which is not beautiful is removed or replaced. The ugly vanishes. Such is Versailles.

The price of Mass paid daily my mornings are my own. And people are kind to me. My father teases me that it is because our family name is so close to that of the King's wife, the Marquise de Maintenon; she is a d'Aubigné and for those not intimate to such things, or those who cannot read, it is assumed we may be blood. Cousin to the wife of the King! A jest of which I do not relieve them, and so I find myself rarely chastised.

But of the day my father tells me I took my first steps with a sword in my hand, but honestly it was a main gauche, a parrying dagger. While his title is Secretary, his task is to oversee the instruction of the use of arms for those who attend to the King's stable; the lieutenants and the grooms of the Black Guard and the Grey Guard—the Musketeers of the Royal Household—and of course the Swiss Guard, who keep the palace itself. It is Father who sees to the employment of the fencing masters from Spain and Italy, and the Low Countries where the men are French and Spanish and something else altogether, all at once. Even de Liancourt has taught at the salle here.

But at my father's side, and to his amusement, I learned all the steps of Thibault's circle; of how to take the measure of my opponent, to find the sentiment of his blade. To feint and rebuff, to press and refuse, to parry and to retort. Further, we learned in the "old way," with heavier rapiers and the grip of the forefinger along the blade, rather than like a pistol, wrapped 'round the guard. Because the weapon is heavier, it is slower, and the movements more deliberate. This way a smallsword, like those worn at court, seems a slighter thing, a quicker thing.

The bravos who come and learn at my father's piste are strong; the sons of strong families, and rich. They shove their youth and their muscle into the weapon and end up flailing about. My father will face them with a baton, or a crop, and disarm them with little effort. Broad shoulders are of no use with the smallsword, and serve only to make you a wider target, and I have learned to take my time. Wrists, not shoulders. Steps, not leaps. And always the eyes on the eyes, with a softened gaze so as to take in the posture, the position, the point, and the measure.

For the new boys I am something of a curiosity in my father's salle. I train in breeches or skirts as it suits me, and while my father forbids that I take challenges, we drill and pass and riposte all in a line, and those who look at me when they should be watching their opponent or their master, pay a quick enough price, delivered by baton or epee.

I have several swords. One a gift from my father, which is a delicate gilt little thing I dare not scratch against another blade; and on such days when it amuses the King that the girls dress in boy's breeches (and there are such days) I have worn it at my side, but never drawn it.

I have two swords that I keep beneath my bed. Both of these are claimed. Or stolen. I suppose one could see it that way. There are swords enough at my father's piste, so I leave mine in my room. My maids are sworn to silence, and do not mention them when they are down there with warmer or chamber pot.

Come to think of it, these grand books of letters do not seem to mention the things under a young lady's bed. This is no doubt deliberate, as everyone I know keeps all manner of things under there. Forbidden books. Small treasures from suitors, or attempted suitors. Childhood things that would be tossed away, like worn-through night dresses softer than new linens. There is likely a book to be written of the secret things under the beds of the young girls of Paris.

I was born in the old Palace, and we moved here when I was two, while the new stables were under construction and my father here to supervise. Behind us there was all marsh, and then forest with a ridge of pines, and then farmland. It is an endless garden now, but I would play with the children from the farms when the borders of the Royal grounds were less distinct.

But still, it is a short ride south to the countryside, where the air is less close, and more honest. The air here is heavy with incense or perfume. I am told the King bathes in perfume twice a day, as the Marquise does not like the stink of his sweat—all those heavy brocades and silks, and candles everywhere, even during the day. So, he sweats, and he reeks, and he douses in perfume. There! A bit of Court gossip at last.

—◄●►—

More gossip, then.

Although not of the King, but of me myself. As I am sixteen, I am expected to be someone's fiancée, and likely someone's lover besides. To be a proper mistress strikes me as a somewhat better situation than a wife. And of the young lieutenants—supple and flawless and stupid—well they are for taking to one's heart or one's bed, but not the altar. Thus far, where my friends have dalliances and proposals, I have merely the disapproving looks of my father, which serves to keep the young men of any intention at a distance. It is likely because they know how easily, as fencing master, he could kill them.

Duelling of course is illegal. The King has decreed it thus. But training too is decreed—a lifetime of rehearsal for that which there is to be no performance—and an accident in my father's salle is a simple thing to orchestrate.

But the one man of whom my father dare not disapprove is his Master, Louis. Not the King, the Count. And the Count has noticed me, in a way of no difference to me and no end of displeasure to my father.

Some weeks ago, they were speaking, the Count and my father, while descending the white stairs to the stables. I was sitting at the bottom, and I cannot recall doing much of anything, honestly. But I rose, as I was expected to rise, and the Count kissed my hand as he has since ceased to kiss my cheek when I was a child, but as he withdrew, his gaze lingered for a heartbeat and a dark cloud came over my father. I smiled and bobbed in the way I have practiced and performed countless times, and perhaps too, I added a little throwaway, like the slightest pinch of the fingers or a slower drift to the eyes. Nothing, really. Just games. But this seemed to have hooked something.

And now he seeks me out. Again, I am doing nothing of anything. Not reading, between Mass and a meal, so simply meandering, and the Count is there around a corner in the garden that it is natural to expect me to turn. He draws me close, saying something that was nothing, and I smell his breath. Like an old man, but not so old, and not so unpleasant. He makes to kiss me, and so I rebuke him, of course, and give him my cheek as I had when I was barely walking and he some vague uncle.

And then his arm comes around and he tries to squeeze my bum.

Not that he can find it really, in this dress. The emerald silk with the blue and yellow stripes, like a Borgia from an old painting, and the fabric is so stiff I could hide a goat under there and he'd be none the wiser. But still, he certainly intends to grab my bum, because he thinks he can.

I consider biting him.

I think, I could pretend to kiss him and just bite his bottom lip and tear it off with my teeth. Or I could fold my fan and drive the hinge right under the pulse of his jaw, open him like a purse full of blood, and leave him gagging for breath in the garden, clutching at the gravel as I watched.

I could do that. It has never occurred to me how terribly simple a man is to open, even before, even after my first blood and the first time I'd cut a boy.

And here is the Count of Armagnac, of the Royal Household, Squire to the King. And I could snuff him like a candle, if I wanted. And I have every right to want to.

But I do not.

I think, I am to be lover to my father's Master. To the Count, although I'm sure there's a Countess somewhere, I've never thought to ask and I'm sure I've never seen her. Squirreled away in some Chateau in the country, squeezing out babies while addressing the pleas of tenants. Managing cooks and rents and throwing whatever parties they might throw outside of Paris, if anyone could even attend such a thing.

I think it was the confidence in his motion. I give him credit for that. He seemed not to care about my reaction at all, and in truth I had none. But he reached for me like a candlestick, or a spoon. Just a thing on his table. I could hate him for that, but for both of us it seemed a practicality for me not to. For him I suppose I am a pretty thing he has a right to take as he will. And for my part I imagine being a Count's mistress would give me a degree of remove from my father's gaze. I am not in want of anything, but I am, it seems, desperately curious. And, I think, I could always kill him later, for daring to think of me as a spoon.

So now we are dancing, Louis and I, after a fashion. I suspect that neither of us particularly care to, but the musicians have begun, and others are watching.

I do not know what the next move is to be, and likely I shall have to invent some.

Honestly if this game were any easier, it would be tedious.

A dinner, and my bristling father at my side like a saddle to a mare, glowering the whole time. And Louis, my Louis now, I suppose, with his slow smiles and just enough lechery in his glances to amuse me.

I laugh and ignore in turn, while the men fill their bellies with wine and we girls play card games. The musicians are fine, and it seems we may run out of places on which to perch candles, so the footmen will simply stand with candelabras. I wear my tangerine dress, and a pearl net in my hair to advertise my innocence.

The room is honey drizzled over marzipan. The walls cream-white, and little tendrils of gold fall across every panel and ledge. There is a spinet to match, no doubt inlaid with ivory and carved with some pastoral scene, a girl on a swing, and cherubs. This room may not have existed a week ago, and may disappear a week from now—a wall moved, the theme restated, fashion being what it is. For this evening, it is small, excessive, and damnably hot.

A small cheer from another table. Someone else is winning tonight, it seems.

A swirl of silk, and a parting (or dismissal) of girls reveals a seated dowager, clearly centuries-old and dusty, held together only by face powder. I glance away to avoid her rheumy eyes, but it is too late, and she feebly beckons me over. Her hands are spider webs, and it is a miracle that the servants have not yet whisked her away with a broom by accident. Dutifully, and knowing full well I am under surveillance at such affairs, I attend to her.

She examines me like a table setting and finds me satisfactory.

The d'Aubigny girl, she says.

Yes, Madame, I reply softly, so as to not disintegrate her with my voice.

I've watched you. We are not so dissimilar, you and I.

I try not to let the thought of it repulse me visibly. She chuckles, or means to.

You could be queen of this place, she says, if you bide your time. Learn patience, play their little games. No, you would have no equal.

Yes, Madame. Thank you, Madame.

I'm not simply saying that, you know, she insists.

Of course not, Madame.

I had my day, my girl, she says wistfully. I had my day.

Of course, I think the Roman Empire had its day, too, and this must have been roughly the same time. But I say nothing. Mercifully, the painted skeleton has her gaze drawn away by something else she finds important to weigh in on, even if that weight is an ounce. I make my escape with a curtsy she does not see.

Louis seems hesitant tonight, perhaps the wine keeps him hovering over the decision I was sure we had made together. Perhaps my costume is too effective? Again, the glance, and the hunger, yes, but so too a distance, as if it could all be brushed aside as a harmless compliment paid to a too-young girl, devoid of intent. Flattery in ardor's stead.

Well, enough of that.

Just as in fencing, the trick is to read the position of the body, to mirror your opponent so that you first anticipate and then dictate his moves. For me this is a chin, and a hand, and a shoulder. And when my fingers trace the lines of my dress, his fingers move not by any will of their own. And I look at him and he does not look away, and I smile and he smiles and then he nods, and laughs.

But then the evening takes a curious turn.

Louis advances, as I knew he would, but in tow he brings both my father and an older gentleman with kind eyes and an outdated wig, a Monsieur La Maupin; *maupin* like the pine trees on the ridge above the farmland. It seems a very deliberate introduction, and I am my most chaste of selves as I let him take my hand.

I speak so softly I can scarcely hear myself. All this pleases my father tremendously, but what is even more remarkable was that not half an hour later the entire performance is repeated with the same actors: Again, the Count brings over M. La Maupin for an introduction, and again I am as decorative and nonsensical as I can make myself, and again my father clucks approval. It all seems as though it was to ensure that such an introduction had actually taken place, and more importantly was *seen* to have taken place. When I think I have fathomed the simplicity of men, they are more simple still. I make a note to extend them even less credit in the future.

The game resumes.

Louis had it seen to that my father should be called away, and that one of the ladies in attendance would surely act as my chaperone? Upon my father's exit, my chaperone giggles and is whisked away by some gallant, my glass filled near to the brim.

Louis takes my arm, and we leave the casino to chatter and music. I admire the way he flicks his fingers at his attendants, so they would not follow us. Not a rehearsed gesture, just a familiar one, and such a modest expenditure of effort.

The light is less riotous here in the brown hall. Even the mirrors have some sepia stipple upon them, meant to invoke what exactly I'm not sure, but it does cut down on the sometimes dizzying reflections of the other halls, and of course there are fewer candles. Only a candelabra every few paces, and only the most inconsequential of servants outside the odd doorway, silent and still.

When Louis tries to kiss me I do not stop him. There is wine and the taste of face powder on his mouth. Kissing him makes him smaller to me somehow, and younger. In my child's mind I had assumed him to be older than my father, because of his station, but he still has the echoes of youth in his manner. I swear if my father or his wife or the King himself happens upon us this moment, he would still have kissed me, because he wanted to. And I let him, mostly because I don't care, and I see now that there is power in that.

The kiss ends abruptly, either because he is a fickle man or he is simply done kissing me, and he strides down the hall. I follow, because it seems right to me. I am likely expected to return to the small party, or perhaps he expects that I would hesitate. I do no such thing and walk at my own pace to wherever he is going.

When we reach the chamber, the door is unattended, the fire and candles inside lit. There is the bed, oak posters burnished to a sheen, and heavy bedclothes in sapphire and gold.

A simple thing to a girl raised around horses. Almost conversational, although we say nothing. We had already agreed, silently that day in the garden, that I was the mistress of the Count of Armagnac, and the bed is merely a wax seal on paper, so we cut the contract into an indenture, and keep our halves.

When it is finished (no pain, no blood, what was I expecting? To hell with the gossip of maids, I tell you this right now), Louis turns to me and says, do you like him? I am not sure what he means. But he refers to M. La Maupin, the older gentleman with the kind eyes from the party.

Louis gives me a small brooch, a pretty gold lace thing with small sapphires, and tells me it is from M. La Maupin.

He thinks to marry you, Louis says.

I tell him that I thought as mistress to the Count I should be excused from such things. He smiles tightly and sort of grunts, explaining that it is no good for a married man to have an unmarried mistress, and that I am to understand.

He tells me to return to the party and wait, and that he will send an escort to see me home, clear across the palace to our family apartments behind the stables. The Palace is almost empty when the King is away, and the halls as dangerous as any alley in the city. Which would not concern me if I could walk armed, like a man.

So now I am home and seen to, my father still away or perhaps seeing to his mistress, who, now, I assume must have a husband. And all the intricate clockwork of the thing seems open to me, each winding and ticking and spinning, all moving the hands 'round, second by second. Had I expected the commonplace to be unfamiliar? That this night-dress and this room would be transformed, as I had assumed I would be? But no, nothing is different, and yet everything.

By my choices, I at sixteen have declared myself a woman. And in doing so I have chosen myself a life.

Well, then.

More about the Monsieur La Maupin of Sainte-Germaine-en-Laye. He is from some Chateau west of the city, where the King was born, and supposedly it is very grand, with a theatre of note. He is responsible for the administration of certain taxes, although I am not sure if that is off in the wilds somewhere or in the city. And he was investigated during the Affair of the Poisons—I do not remember it, as I was very small, but it still clouds the air here. A plot to assassinate the King, using potions and black magic. Courtiers turned on one another in a frenzy of accusation, secrets and scandals exposed, and there was torture, and confession, and death.

The affair had made a celebrity of de La Reynie, the Lieutenant General of Police. Mercifully, he does not live at the Palace, for I've seen him only twice and I swear there is in him a howling northern wind where others have a soul. If the poor Monsieur was interrogated by such a disease as de La Reynie and survived, he must be made of firmer steel than he appears.

My Louis has sent me a cloak of the richest black taffeta. It has a deep hood, so that it conceals my face even from alongside. It is anonymity in silk. At night I turn my back on the palace, always shining, always ablaze in the dark, and peering from my silken cave I see the stars sharper than I've ever witnessed them. But this is the King's design. All light must come from himself, from the Palace, so bright it outshines all other lights.

It is probably treason to turn one's back on such a light, and to look at the stars so.

Our nights are all wrapped up in small parties and performances. Sometimes we dance and we are expected to excel at ballet, or singing, or an instrument, although I have no patience for the latter.

There are the plays for women; these are mostly silly and for practice, but still we rehearse. There are costumes, and the same musicians that play for the King, but not the ones who accompany him. At these, some imperfections are tolerated, and very young girls will often dance here and show their aunts and nodding grandmothers what they have learned.

There are the smaller household plays, and these are properly on stage, with painted scenes and elaborate costumes, and most of these are done seasonally. Here the audiences have sterner brows; the bar is set quite high, and a misstep or a missed note is met with audible disapproval. The expectations of the girls are severe, and it is not uncommon to see tears backstage before and after, and even during, a performance.

But the Royal household plays, these are an altogether different thing. The King is informed, but never invited, as it is his house, and he may go where he chooses. But there is always a great chair, set well up in front of the stage, and the chair seems to radiate a kind of presence. Beside this usually vacant chair, is one ever so slightly smaller and less sumptuous, but still a finer thing than we shall ever sit in. And thereupon sits the Marquise, as a kind of monitor to ensure that the Palace's expectations of perfection and beauty are maintained.

Behind her though are the ranks of zealots, in their flat, black frocks and lace collars. Stern, unsmiling, and clutching peasant-rosaries and small bibles. They are there to ensure there is no lewdness or impropriety, despite the fact that that is precisely what the composers have in mind.

Ignoring the grim row of black jackdaws, I do adore these evenings. People are attentive to every detail, to the lacing of a shoe and even the coiling of a rope. Everything measured, patient, intentional with not even the entertainment of error. I am not so meticulous in any other aspect of my life, but for the stage everything must be perfect, and I delight in that. It is like a violin string—taut and in tune. And here is where I make my music.

It is a simple enough thing to get away with— to enter the stage with a chorus of girls, all identically costumed, each step absolutely in time and identical, and yet still stand out. The other girls are counting under their breath and worrying about a stray hair or a missed cue, but it has always been effortless for me to simply assume the role and its nature. Whether I am to be a swan or a sylph or some characteristic—often "Virtue" or the "Voice of Pride"—one is simply that, and nothing else. Not pretending. Becoming.

Then you have them. And then you can play. Then this swan or sylph or virtue will catch the eye of that one young man in the third row. And again, so yes, it was you, and I see the smile and gesture. And you ignore him through the second act so that he's discouraged, or doubting himself, and again with a flash of the eyes you have sought him out and see how he burns like a candle in his seat. But of course, you are blameless, because you have made each identical step and spoken each identical word from the chorus. You have done nothing. Yet you have done everything.

And later when he enquires, he will be informed that she who has intrigued him so is the mistress of the Count of Armagnac, cousin to the King, the girl herself quite possibly the cousin of the Marquise by rumour, and a creature altogether removed from the realm of possibility. But before that little victory, there is applause.

Applause has flavour. There is a thundering bass note, like chocolate or coffee. There is a mild, smooth mid note, like cake or cream. And there is a light and spicy sweetness to the finish, like sugar or peppers from the New World. I am becoming a connoisseur of applause and am learning to read it more carefully. There is a different taste to appreciation of the story, or the composer, or the performance itself. There is the reward for a joke, usually at the expense of someone present, and hopefully for the black clad zealots who hover above the King's wife like a storm cloud. And then there is the reward for the singer, always a soprano, who is given a solo to make them all fall in love with her.

As a contralto, there are no solos for me.

—— ◖●◗ ——

At night, one of Louis' men comes for me.

I am still in my father's apartments, though he is rarely here. It seems my role as his master's mistress has given me a distance only of the heart, and not of oversight. I may eventually be moved into the Palace proper, into the Count's apartments (the King has moved all the nobility and their households here to keep an eye on them), but not until I am married. Apparently, I cannot be seen to be carrying on with another woman's husband until I have marriage vows of my own to break.

But I am summoned, so I make them wait. I of course know when I am expected; there is always a flurry of the news of maids hours before any alarm at the door.

I am sure to sport any gift or token he has recently sent me. I have learned the dresses he likes and the colours he prefers and the perfumes that please him, simply because this is the costume of the part I have assumed. And then in a motion well-rehearsed, my huge black taffeta cloak around my shoulders. I descend the stairs and raise the deep hood instead of acknowledging my escort.

He bears a lantern even though it is bright enough outside for a jeweler to work. I am invisible although all can see me. We are discreet even though everyone knows where we are going. I am escorted even though I walk ahead of him.

The maids at first wanted to accompany me, but I am not so sheltered to know that where I am invulnerable, they are not. No man, and certainly no man's man, would dare lift a finger or an incautious word against a daughter of the Royal household. But the girls of lower rank, and servants—no, I would not have a girl stand in the halls of the palace outside my door. Such girls are simply plucked away, like breadcrumbs for crows.

Tonight, there is a different man. Handsome, broad and cocky, though this was in his walk and not his manners. His body is slashed across by a great swath of leather, a baldric, and buckled to that was no smallsword, but a basket hilted sidesword.

That is no duelling weapon, I say.

No, Mademoiselle, he answers.

I ask to see it and he hesitates, but I tell him I am not so foolish as to cut off my own head with it, and he draws it and hands it to me. It has a pommel in the shape of a cat's head, with small, pointed ears.

A *schiavona*, I say. Venice.

Indeed, Mademoiselle, and something about me knowing steel that may be innuendo. I take a few steps and cut the air with the great heft of the thing, although the weight was in the hand and not the blade. Beautifully balanced, and the candlelight shows bites in the steel that are clearly not from mere practice. I hand it back to him with thanks and he brings me to our rendezvous.

Louis is preoccupied tonight. I dare not ask, and my purpose is to distract him from such things. He asks again, as he does each time, if I have heard from M. La Maupin, and again I say I have not. This seems to concern him, but not overmuch. I think he merely wishes it were otherwise.

I have at last received a letter from M. La Maupin. A few pages of nothing, a small hand for a man, and then this:

"…endeavor to serve you dutifully as husband."

So that is that. He has spoken to my father, then, and made arrangements, and this has been brought to the King—no one in the household is to be married without his personal consent.

Madame La Maupin. This woman I have become is to have a name.

The grass is pale gold, chill and dew-wet from dawn.

How did I come to be here? I must have called this boy out—there is no reason for him to do likewise to me. Unless there is a reason and wine has stolen it from me. Regardless.

He is nervous. So, so nervous, and chiding himself for it. He sees only a girl, in a white shift, in grass of pale gold, with a smallsword in her hand. Clearly at some point he contemplated killing me, or I him I suppose, or he wouldn't be here. Here in the grass, an hour past dawn.

He takes the only form he knows: sword foot forward, blade parallel to the ground from stiffened shoulder, knuckles to the sky and his off-hand dangling rather strangely but at least in front of his heart.

The wind comes up and teases some hair from the ribbon. Too early for wigs. Sensible. Still, he does not want to be here, but honour in the wake of some drink-fueled comment besmirching his honour or another's, therefore his by proxy...and here we are.

I am in first position, relaxed. I even close my eyes to feel the early sun, just to unsettle him. Left hand practically on hip, my sword guard almost but not quite resting on the left wrist, blade pointed to the ground. I could level it at his throat half an hour before his lunge landed, from that distance. No measure, this boy.

I raise an eyebrow. He does not flinch at this, though he should.

I reach the blade out to him, fully extended, and he goes to parry it, but of course it's nowhere near him, so he has to stretch to catch it.

The tiniest of circles is all it takes to remove my point from his attack. A half step, and now the point is eight or so inches closer to his face. I relax in this position, which I can hold for hours. I *have* held it for hours, in my father's salle, at risk of the baton were I to slack or drop guard even for the flutter of an eyelash.

He reaches again to strike my blade, though this forces his knee over his foot. I let him take the tick of the gesture, and this sound and modest shock gives me the sentiment, the feel of the blade and its weight and his grip and his resolve. His breathing is already ragged, his throat dry.

I thought him pretty moments before. But now he is too clumsy, too unkempt. An uncoiled rope.

I attack his shoulder, knowing he will over-compensate on the parry and leave his breast unguarded. Though when I extend to his left he parries again, yet wildly, and steps out of measure.

Very well. He will be back.

He gathers his breath, and resumes his single, practiced form.

I attack his right hip, his parry swinging awkwardly low. Stepping in, I bind his blade down and out of the way, swatting his right ear hard with my left hand, and stepping back out of his reach lest he has the sense to drop his sword and simply tackle me—a strategy with likely more success than his current one.

I have insulted him, and I shouldn't laugh, so I make an effort not to.

He lunges for me, too straight and too stiff. Easy enough to simply lean out of the way. He hops back and does exactly the same move again; oddly, to the same spot, which by now I'm nowhere near.

I slap his blade away near perpendicular. But he's emboldened by the sound of steel on steel, and pivots, and for the first time engages my blade. He is undisciplined, but I'm seeing some blood in him at least.

He realizes that he is stronger than me and thinks if he can more or less punch the air between us with the guard of his sword, that he will overpower me. As though I were on the edge of a cliff and had nowhere to go. But this is a big meadow.

It's more of a tiny valley, really, between two green swards barely the height of my head. I thought this might give the matter a degree of privacy. Still, I could retreat for hours were I so inclined, and he would be so winded we would need to break for lunch.

Which reminds me that I ought to have had breakfast.

I am nearly punished for my inattention, as he's closed some measure between us. Stepping back, and stepping in again, light as the dancer I am, I thrust first an imbrocatta to his high guard, then roll my hand 'round, palm skywards, to a stocatta, under his arms. I'm not close enough to wound him, just to tap the pommel of his sword with a troubling tick, which causes him to retreat.

But then everything changes. There is a glint of steel above the green rise, and another, and another all in a row. Everything changes, everything changes forever lost in that forest of halberds. The Swiss Guard.

My servants or his have betrayed us. Or whomever was in shouting distance when this duel was called, I honestly have no memory of it. Yet here we are, arrested, and everything has changed, forever.

A man-shaped thing, I think to myself. A man-shaped thing behind a gloriously expensive desk, beneath a massive black wig.

Man-shaped, yes, fit enough. Certainly fashionable. Yet not a man, for a man has a soul you can see in his eyes. The eyes of the Lieutenant General of the Police give no such indication. Whatever humanity once resided there has been long ago evicted.

Monsieur, I protest and pretend, I'm certain that–

Certain of what? de La Reynie interrupts. Certain that a daughter of the palace can disregard the King's law by duelling?

He has been standing, silhouetted by the grid of the window that now evokes the bars of a cage. An iron gate between myself and the shining world outside. He sits with purpose.

Are you aware, he continues calmly, of the identity of the boy you were about to kill?

I think of him, there in the meadow, in his fawn-coloured breeches and white chemise, his blond hair pulled back in a thin silk ribbon. No name presents itself to recollection.

No, Monsieur Lieutenant General, I admit. But it was merely sport, Monsieur. He had no intention–

Of harming you? he interrupts again. No, I suspect not, nor the ability if he harboured such intention. However, I suffer no illusion that you are entirely capable of killing him.

He is right, of course. The boy's technique was nonexistent. He met me at dawn more expecting a kiss than a murder, it is now apparent. Neither of us thought to bring seconds. The whole thing was rather ridiculous.

At least I am not in prison. I assume the boy is. Instead, I am at the Palace proper, in this rather extravagant room for a policeman's office. Though they have not served me cake. Will he kill me if I try to leave?

Can I kill him first? I would have to strike without looking at him. I fear him, I admit this to myself. The coldness of his eyes. A calculating cruelty. For the first time in my life, I consider begging. Or bargaining, which I suppose is as close as I am likely to get.

Monsieur—I begin.

I know who you are, Mademoiselle. I have observed you for quite some time. You have an interesting set of skills.

Monsieur? I say, genuinely confused. Perhaps he has heard me sing?

He begins: You have insinuated yourself, via your father's position, into the Count's household. You are more capable than many with a blade; certainly more capable than one would expect. You are also not as naive as you pretend.

I simply nod now, curious.

It does seem that you are something of a curiosity, he says. A dangerous one.

Again, a nod, his comment a flattery to which I am not completely immune.

My intention, he continues, and therefore your alternative to justice, is to make you dangerous for the right people. For the good of the King.

The right people? I ask.

Or the wrong people. Regardless. In the course of management of various affairs, it would be... useful to have some elements removed from time to time. This can be done through innuendo, through rumour. Occasionally I should expect you to perform as courier, discreetly. I imagine your upbringing has prepared you thoroughly for such tasks.

Of course it has, I think. The flurry of love-notes and scandal, of whispers and the politics of skirts? Second nature.

To what end, Monsieur? I inquire.

To my end, my dear girl, he says. I do not like the way he says it.

And would this removal, I press, go beyond the assassination of reputations?

From time to time, he says dismissively. Were a gentleman at the palace, or in the city, through sport, as you say, fall to misadventure, at the hands of a girl... well, unfortunate, surely, and tragic for the family. But blameless. Sport, as you say.

You wish me to duel, despite the King's law? I know what he intends, but I insist he says it.

Only those whom I say, yes. A certain pardon, in advance of the matter, is granted.

You want me to spy for you, kill for you, I illustrate. But only those whom you chose to die. And in so killing, make myself appear incompetent at sport, and thereby innocent.

See? he says brightly. Not so naive, as I have said.

I tell him I am no street thug to garotte his enemies in the alleys.

Ah, he says, But I have enough of those. You, you Mademoiselle, are something altogether special.

Your *special* street thug, I reply.

If you like, he says.

I must admit I do not, I tell him. And I don't.

Or, he offers, we can simply set aside this conversation after your sentencing. A major offense, to draw a blade against a man under the protection of the King.

We were merely practicing—I begin once more.

I have witnesses to the contrary. And if you like, I can find a hundred witnesses to say you threatened the King, that you spouted wings and flew, that you breathed fire. Now, calm yourself, child. I have little interest in pursuing this course unless you leave me no choice.

Leaving you no choice by declining your offer, I rebuke.

As you say, he agrees.

I am to be your pet assassin, on a leash of silk ribbon, I suggest.

If you care to see it that way, he admits, it would not be to your detriment.

Monsieur, I say, rising... and then make some comment about a chamber pot, the eventual destination of its contents and his inevitable discomfort.

I leave. He does not kill me.

I should have had breakfast.

As I leave his office, the guard outside meets my fuming gaze. I recognize him as one of the halbard-bearers who arrested me earlier. His broken nose looked better in the garish livery of the Swiss Guard than it does in the dull brown of his civilian garb.

Shots at dawn. Muskets! It is the Black Musketeers, in advance of the King's return. While the sound terrifies the maids and sets the spaniels to barking, I find it thrilling.

There are two kinds of black at the Palace: the drab, flat black of the zealots who surround the Marquise (and increasingly the King); and the deep, shimmering blacks of the musketeer's velvets. One is an absence of colour, light itself washed away from the world. The other is a mystery, exciting, like hiding in a wardrobe as a child with your heart racing for fear of capture.

The Black Musketeers were the guards of the King's enemy, a Cardinal long dead, and so the King made them his own out of spite. Now they are France's finest sons, skilled and rich and beautiful. There is also the Grey Musketeers, the Queen's Guard, but France has no Queen. Only the King's secret wife, about whom no one is supposed to know but everyone does, and must, to survive.

Jean-Baptiste. That is the name of my husband-to-be. No one has told me until now.

Today is my wedding day. Father comes to say kind words. His mistress too came to kiss me upon the cheek. Earlier Mama was here, and wept. In fact all the women of the house weep, and scurry like hens, because with all the thousand things there are to do in a household, a wedding means another thousand more.

I shall miss this room. I do not suppose I shall have cause to see it again.

━━◖●◗━━

It is nearly three hours to the city by carriage. Quicker to walk, I think. A great deal of time is spent attempting to encourage others to get out of the way. Each quarter mile is welcome air between myself and de La Reynie and his schemes.

As of this morning I am Madame La Maupin. I am a new creature, with a new name, a name I had not heard even a month ago except in reference to the pines south of the Palace.

The wedding was simply morning Mass, although better attended. Louis was there, ensuring that all was executed to his satisfaction. He wore a blue in the Italian style, lighter and brighter, because he knew it would make me happy, even though I suppose I ought to feel some sadness at this, marrying a man who is not my lover.

All was halted in an instant upon the arrival of the King. The priest's hands frozen in the air like a puppet suspended. The King spoke discreetly to the Count, cousin to cousin, one Louis to another. I wondered in that moment that if the King were to cancel the wedding if I was to be disappointed, or not. But he turned and left, and I am to understand there are wedding presents upon my arrival in the city, where Jean-Baptiste keeps apartments.

We have barely spoken, my husband and I. Me to a deck of cards stuttering about the carriage table and he to his papers. He makes an apology, but there are pressing matters, he says, and we will talk over dinner.

I wonder if Louis will take a lover while I am in the city. And I wonder if he will think of me at all.

This carriage is awkward as it lurches from side to side. Uncomfortable. Never before have I been such a bird in a cage.

But the light is beautiful through the trees, and somewhere there are church bells tolling. I can barely make them out through the clop and rattle, but I can still hear them.

We approach the river.

So it seems my husband is not to exert his rights on this our wedding night. Very well.

He is a gentleman of excellent manners and kindness, although he repeatedly apologizes—a trait I find wearisome. I was not sure of what to expect here. His—our, I suppose now—apartments are an hour from the river, making it over four hours from the Palace, and I am sore from the carriage-ride. Less than an hour on horseback, I am certain, and my back would not ache so.

The space is clean but dull, and precisely what a bachelor tax-something-or-other would keep in the city. The place is kept by staff who are not fashionable, but it does not smell as bad as the street, and I am grateful for this.

I should redecorate. I could plan parties to my liking and sing Italian whenever I wished. I will change the draperies from the heavy reds and brown (brown!) to pale golds and pinks and greens, the colour of spring shoots. If I am to be the Madame of a house, let it be a colourful house, with fine music.

But right now, I crave sleep more than anything. My thoughts blur in of the sounds of the street, different and the same as Palace life—shouting, horses, drunkenness.

———◦●◦———

The game I play today is to pretend I shall be playing it forever. A longer breakfast instead of Mass, and an address to the staff. Jean-Baptiste has been called away and left a note saying that the household staff was at my disposal, which means apparently looking at bills from butchers and fish-mongers and candlemakers.

Can this be different? I ask the maître.

Different in what way, Madame? he answers.

And so of course I say in every way. Different fish. Different flowers. Different cakes. I mean to do the entire household.

I send him to bring me cloth merchants, and wig makers, and florists, and cutlers and furniture makers. I wish to see swatches and drawings. He nods without speaking, which is a blessing because his breath is terrible. How does one tell one's servants they have terrible breath? Surely at the palace there is someone responsible for ensuring it is not so, some ancient protocol in effect. I imagine them all lined up in the morning, breathing at the command of some undersecretary for pleasant breath with a royal charter going back in his family for centuries, dispensing cloves like communion bread into the waiting mouths of offenders. And no such expertise available to me. I fear a misstep.

But not for long.

It is not, I decide, all that different from putting on a play. I am creating a stage. An ambience. The walls here are of grey stone behind white plaster and dingy tapestries. Not tasteless, simply masculine. But these are colours of winter, of age, and I'll have none of it. I want spring, spring everywhere. I shall get a pet rabbit, so that here in the city within the bone-white boxes of apartments I shall have a garden in every room.

But of course, even the play is a play, and here I am pretending to be Madame La Maupin when I am, in reality, the mistress of the Count of Armagnac, and in a week or an hour he will send for me, and I will abandon my husband for my lover.

Or I could stay. The city is changing, or so they say, and I'm sure I could get over the stink. The King has ordered new gardens, new theatres. Surely there is a part for me?

But looking out narrow windows to winding streets, all is grey as the sea. As bright as I could make this flat, it would still be a raft in the ocean of Paris. And there is my shining island of Versailles to return to.

Jean-Baptiste will play his part, enter and exit as he is bade, and I am to be summoned to a different stage altogether. If I am to be a woman in this world of men and their arrangements, then I am decided to be such a woman the likes of which they have never seen, God help them.

———◄●►———

As expected, my husband has made his excuses and must leave the city, suggesting I "visit family" in his absence. This no doubt the machinations of Louis. What currency among men is exchanged, that one abandons one's wife so?

I have dined well enough, but I am not in the habit of asking for things; a slice of fruit or almond cake— these things were always about. But in my home I have to consider them, and ask for them, and have them brought to me. Bizarre!

So, without so much as buying pillows I leave my house, my raft, in Paris and return to Versailles, the very center of the universe, the jewel of the world.

And so, to the great homecoming, the long concourse of finely crushed gravel, raked even in the carriage's passing by footmen in short wigs whose task it is to stand and wait and rake, and stand and wait.

The Palace dazzles. The light is caught by the glass of a thousand windows and tossed back to me like a ball. The driver takes me to the Palace proper, and not the stables. I am met by footmen and two girls who are to be my maids. I do not recognize them, but that is no mystery. The other side of the Palace is a world away, and how many servants here? A thousand? I have no idea. The farms of France must be emptied of girls, each here brought and taught to bob and fetch silently, ignoring the filth of chamber pots and questionable sheets, snoring and scandal.

I am now ensconced in the rooms where I first presented my virtue (the absurdity of this phrase!) to Louis. A bedroom right off the hall, with rooms adjacent. It does mean that visitors must cross my bedroom before being seated in my salon, but the sitting room is too small to accommodate the great boat of a bed, a giant dark thing, centuries-old with tapestries of crimson and silver thread.

But a room of my own, in the Palace proper.

I feel the need to walk the halls. I am stiff and sore from the carriage, and would run for running's sake, if I could.

My father is here and introduced me to some Polish gentlemen visiting court. They have presented a pair of the most magnificent pistols to the King, by way of the Secretary to the Master of Horse. I have never seen the equal of these weapons; gilt and worked, yes, but they are wheel locks with the precision of miniature clocks, and a pale steel barrel the length of my forearm.

It amuses them, I think, to hand such things to a woman. I take one in each hand, marvel at the fit and heft of them. They almost laugh as I take pretend aim, first at a distant wall, and then one of the Poles himself. He does not like the look in my eye, and I do my best not to smirk returning the pistols to their silk-lined box.

While my father bowed deeply and apprecia-tively, these will never see flint to powder, however the King fancies himself a soldier. No, these will disappear into one of the great galleries of similar diplomatic gifts, neglected, along with thousands of snuffboxes and fans and chests; the whole world sending beauty to the Sun King, only to have such beauty neglected. The King wants only French beauty, and even then only that of his own doing.

Waking to the maids, who stand with folded linens, hot water in a basin. The fire lit, which I didn't hear. The poor things must be freezing, or perhaps not with all the running around they have to do. A tray of letters I reach for when my arm is scarcely through my sleeve.

Still no Louis. Perhaps the bloom is off my rose?

A day on the piste, in my father's salle. Smallsword.

The bravos choose the same stance: erect, shoulders in line, sword foot forward, guard high. I find this guard exhausting, and besides I do not have the reach to lunge so. No, for me, my sword foot is well back, so that I can step and add a good yard to my lunge. So, my guard must be in fourth position; low to cover my exposed left, pommel to the left hip and the blade diagonal across my body—but always the point leveled at the eyes.

Rare lunges for me but passes. Being smaller I must get past and inside my opponent's point. Further I must often beat his blade as I close distance, to take the sword hand first, and only then the arm, the chest.

We are created well for swordplay. The large muscles on the outside of the body—the arm, the hip, the thigh—are thick and strong, with not so much blood. It is the arteries inside the arm, inside the leg, that are to be protected. A slice to the bicep is nothing, but inside the arm, a cut there will snip the strings of a puppet, with torrents of blood. I have seen a shot go amiss in that very room, a point pierced through and exiting the soft inside of the thigh, the victim drained to white in under a minute, near drowning in a thickening pool of crimson.

A new drill today; wooden daggers, in the style of the fourteenth century master Fiore dei Liberi and his text *The Flower of Battle*, a book I know well from childhood. The illustrations I found comical, with the victor of each pass wearing a little crown levitating above his head.

Most of the men chafe at such study, though not visibly. They prefer smallsword, only smallsword, for that is what they carry, and each harbours a fantasy of running some miscreant through, for the upholding of honour and the reward of affection and reputation. They cannot see the foundation on which their imaginary castles are built.

However, they respect my father, and attend.

A new face—here, at least. de La Reynie's man, with the broken nose. Is he not Swiss Guard? Do they not have their own pistes? Why train here, with the Musketeer's grooms? Unless he is not Swiss Guard, and my arrest some ruse of his Master's devising. Likely.

The dagger work is a tangle, more wrestling than blade play. We practice several disarms, in turn. One involves an elbow-grab and pulling the opponent's dagger through his legs. When I am partnered with the broken-nosed man whom I refuse to recognize, I jab the wooden dowel high up into his groin.

He growls and raises a hand to strike me, but I will not give him the satisfaction of a flinch.

My father chastises me for my clumsiness, and I give him my most innocent apology.

I am slow today and out of practice. We drill, and we drill, and we repeat. But as there are no other lessons for me—married, I am considered a complete creature, merely awaiting the arrival of children—I am free in the meantime to return tomorrow and practice. I do wonder if the man with the broken nose will return to spy on me.

———❬●❭———

Louis comes for me at last. He brings me a necklace from the city, a fine thing of pearls, awaiting a smile or a kiss, so these are offered. He asks if I had lain with Jean-Baptiste, my husband, and I tell him no. He seems almost sad for me. But we take our pleasure here, in my rooms, and it is a different thing, an unhurried thing. I do love him, I think, in my way, though not deliriously so.

He sleeps now. It shall be a curious thing, to awaken to a man.

In the halls after breakfast there is Elise, who trills that she has not seen me since my wedding—as though it were an actual event—and insists we take coffee together. As ever, I accept.

We grew up together, daughters of the Court. While she is no swordswoman, she has been my sparring partner, nonetheless. When to press gossip, and when to withdraw from it, appalled. Elise is the mistress of keeping the upper hand in all social situations and can flatter or devastate in turn. She can make a jest sound like the most innocent comment, and the most glorious praise a pantomime.

She plays games with boys, enough to keep them where she wants them. This and that and no further, so they are always trembling with frustration, a crowd of them buzzing like a hedge full of bees around her, because she wishes it so. When we were young, she confessed she could not wait to play the libertine, perhaps the madame of some glorious Ottoman pleasure palace, with lithe dancers suspended on silks from a glittering dome. It strikes me as not the strangest thing to wish for.

As girls we were in all the household plays together, but it was apparent even then that she had chosen a different stage. These days I see her only ever behind a fan, and that behind a wall of competing musketeers (The Swiss Guards are completely forbidden to the daughters of the Court, so I am certain she maintains several in her possession).

She is beautiful, blond and impeccable, and kisses my cheek with the precision of a wind-up doll.

She is the perfect creature for such a place as this. Intricate and glittering.

Here is a thing as yet unconfessed. The brace of Polish pistols I have taken for myself. They were too beautiful to go to waste, tucked away tagged on a shelf. These I have hidden beneath my bed. Of course.

It is a crime, I admit. But a crime of the liberation of beauty. Such workmanship and intricacy must be given freedom, and life. How I do not know, but they shall have powder and ball and the crack of proper weapons. Someday.

Here is a thing as yet unconfessed. The brace of Polish pistols I have taken for myself. They were too beautiful to go to waste, tucked away tagged on a shelf. These I have hidden beneath my bed. Of course.

I am in love. I can only say this in my own thoughts, this dangerous secret.

Louis is a fool and my father a fool and my husband a fool and I too, am a fool, because I believed that you could move about like a piece on a chessboard and be satisfied for what passes for love.

I cannot.

I met a man, a Southerner in my father's employ. A fencing master named Sérannes. He is beautiful, and strong, like a wild thing. Everything this place mocks and pretends to be, he is. Beautiful. Perfect. Immortal.

I have to kiss him. I've never seen anything like him before in my life. He makes me hesitate. I don't know what to say to him, or what to do with my hands. There is no performance laid out for me, no lines written, when I see him. There is an honesty in his mouth and his eyes and I think he is the most real thing I have ever seen. Everything else is suddenly shabby. Counterfeit.

His laugh is clear and ready, and when he leans, I wish to be that which he leans on. And when he takes up the sword, he moves like a dancer.

Monsieur Sérranes! It is late and I must sleep but I shall dream of you. Be certain of this.

———◄●►———

I make to go and see him today, but not yet set out. Louis arrives mid-morning unannounced.

He is drunk—so much wine at breakfast—and enters my chamber door without announcement. He has a servant girl by the wrist, and his intentions clear enough.

Dramatic to the point of farce he introduces us.

Madame La Maupin, he says with a flourish. And?

Justine, the girl says. Scarcely thirteen, I'm guessing, and terrified. Louis makes to leer at me, but the wine keeps him bleary and blinking. Everything about the moment is dangerous.

Justine, I say, let's have a look at you, and I take both her hands in mine, which makes Louis let go of her.

I can see why he likes you; I tell her. You have very pretty eyes, and a nice chin.

By this point Louis has staggered to the bed, fallen onto it, and farted noisily. But he keeps his eyes on the two of us.

Have you ever been with such a man, my lion, the Count of Armagnac? I ask the girl.

She shakes her head. Nor any man, I'd wager. Boys perhaps.

Do you dance? and she nods quickly. Just a little, she says.

My lion Louis wants a performance, I whisper, but so that Louis could hear me. We shall give him one. But just a taste of what is to follow, yes? For surely, one more pleasing is to require preparations.

Preparations, yes, he says from the bed. Rehearsals.

Costumes! I reply, carrying the game. And music!

No musicians, he says gruffly.

Very well then, I agree, letting go of Justine to stroke her face, keeping her eyes on mine and not the grotesque figure of the drunken Count on my bed. I bow, and she curtsies, and we count an old pavane, and dance in the small space between the door and the bed. Justine nearly trips, and laughs innocently, which wakes Louis up some.

I stop the dance and touch her face once more. I lean in to kiss her, but instead of a peck I take her lips full on mine and feel the girl stiffen with discomfort. Glancing over my shoulder, Louis has missed the whole thing and fallen asleep.

I whisper, you were lucky, and bid her send someone—someone else—for a pitcher of water, a bowl of ice, and a pot of coffee. Cakes and fruit, too.

Now go, I say, and as she curtsies in obedience and thanks, I again take her hand and whisper, this was not your misstep, but never find yourself in this position again. Leave the Palace if you must, make any excuse. Never return. And she stammers some prayer for my kindness and leaves.

Court is no place for such girls. Innocence here is a game. But true innocence is a dangerous thing; a threat to be crushed.

Fuming at my missed chance to see Sérannes, I remove my gown unaided and change again into my morning dress, climbing into bed with Louis, which is expected of me.

I curse him as I pluck off his wig and stroke the dark curls of his hair. He begins snoring softly.

Idiot.

By way of apology, I suppose, Louis sends one of his men here with gifts. A bolt of silk, a white peacock I immediately send away, and a wrapped book.

I have seen these kinds of books before, of course, though as a girl such things are forbidden. Likely as a Christian women they remain so. But it is one of those luridly illustrated things on "the arts of love," almost entirely concerned with how to indulge a man, though there are some very funny drawings of what the Romans were supposed to have got up to.

I'm not sure if I am to be aroused, amused, or insulted!

I go to see him. Monsieur Sérannes.

I know it is him from his walk. Deliberate and measured. Easy and confident. Even the way his sword swings at his hip is like a dream. I daresay I follow him for half the courtyard.

I walk too quickly, or perhaps not quickly enough. For he stops to talk to two girls I recognize but whom I do not know. Gossips the both of them, and one with teeth like a horse. The pair of them flirting outrageously, and without skill.

I dare not approach him after this. When he sees me, I shall arrange for him to see me first.

And me alone.

———◂●▸———

That very night of the afternoon where I saw him with the two terrible girls, I attend a small party to which I almost don't go, but I change my mind at the last minute. I had been practicing a song, and thought it might be ready for a small performance. I take my time with my makeup, as if for the stage, but not quite so much as that.

Arriving late, candles everywhere and the musicians particularly excellent, and then I discover why. Lully! Lully is here, however briefly.

All music in the Palace is Lully. Nothing is hummed or plucked without first playing out on the stage of his imagination. It is Lully who, when the King was a boy, created the King. Not his mother and her dour zealots (who now choke the King's wife in a disapproving fog), but it was Lully who made the Sun King, the Dancing King. Music as a weapon. Nobody on earth ever understood that until Lully, who can write a thousand operas in a day. He was an Italian, until the King made him

French. It is said that if you smashed open every violin in Versailles, you would find the shards of Lully's soul hidden there. He is grey now, but I hear he was beautiful in his youth. There is still fire in his manner though, a certainty of one's own magic, and a modest appraisal of the magic of others. I adore him. How could I not? But the master leaves shortly after my arrival, and some fellows come in, all in the King's Black save for one perfect figure in brown.

How could I love a man in brown? I know! But there he is, tall and lean and perfect, the curls of his hair brushed from his eyes with strong fingers.

I turn because I do not want him to see me before my moment, before my choosing. I speak with one of the musicians, and there are murmurs of approval and they begin, and I take up my song.

And now of course I have him, and Sérannes falls in love with me.

It is a thing of the eyes, the hands, leaning forward and then away, the shoulders the last to move. Singing is dancing. And now I know that singing is lovemaking.

I am not shy as an hour later I retreat to the hall, unescorted. Knowing he would follow. Knowing that I shall kiss him without a word. Why speak, when I had already sung? We were lovers from before this instant.

I had only to send a boy to find my maid and wait for her to fetch my cloak and a few things from my apartments, and send her away again—with each summoning Sérannes expertly turned discreetly and paced to an acceptable distance, just as any of Louis' escorts might.

Because of the season, I knew who would have a vacant apartment—surely Louis would know of all my own comings and goings, and Sérannes is quartered in the block behind the stables, under my own father's shadow. But the palace and I grew up together, and I know these halls as they were built. A girlhood of being chased away by stonemasons and painters gives one a decent map of the place, and we make our way unseen.

And here we remain, three days hidden away. My lover Sérannes sleeps but I want to keep this moment here in memory. The moment I made him fall in love with me.

—◖●◗—

Louis sends for me this morning, early. A maid comes for me, my friend's girl, who has been keeping us in meat and wine, and seems panicked.

I have her fetch my most modest blue dress, a plain thing, and unadorned. This costume I assume, and speed to the closest, most unused chapel (of which the palace has several) and tell the girl to let Louis know I would be there.

As if to underscore my guilt, in the halls I catch sight of de La Reynie, haunting spectre that he is. Come to arrest me for the crime of love, I imagine. But that is ridiculous. Talking to members of his staff, even his voice is like swallowing ice. A cold ache in my gut. I do not meet his eyes and steady my pace. Just a chaste little mouse on my way to the chapel. Invisible.

If he notices me, he says nothing.

Of course, he notices me.

I make my way.

I am surprised to find a priest there, saying a Mass for no one, so I take my most pious steps and make myself a small thing, a penitent thing, rosary in gloved hand.

No image can have been more innocent than the one which Louis finds, and the priest gives no sign that I have just arrived. A skill I learned early on in the household plays—occasionally one must make oneself to be furniture.

He suspects something, but there is some privilege to the mystery of women, and the shelter of the sacraments. He makes to sit beside me at first, but thinks better of it, and simply leaves. I take communion, unforgiven for my sins, which I was taught merely adds to them.

Rather a great number in recent days! Not that I should be proud of them, which too bolsters their accounting.

But I am. Oh, I am.

Sérannes' given name is Bernard. Bernard! An ugly word for so beautiful a man. I have forbidden him to speak it, and he laughed. So for me he is just Sérannes.

Jean-Baptiste has sent for me. Not back to Paris, but to somewhere in the north I've never heard of. His letter arrives in a packet of household business: I am to see to the accounts of the baker and grocer, and the salaries of the staff. It is all nonsensical to me. How are things to be paid? Am I to find loose sous about the palace and send them? I simply sign the sheafs of paper "Mme La Maupin" and return them. There are even little squares of fabric, which I am to choose and about which I had forgotten. They are all wrong, regardless.

But as for my husband, and the north, I shall not go. I should sooner go back to the apartments in the city, where I am to be the mistress of my own house. I would leave Louis and the stink of this place, its choking perfume and the piss in the halls and the constant hammering of workmen that I have known all my life as this great glass cage was erected about me; this magnificent tumor of Versailles.

No carriage for me. I would take Lilas, if I knew the way, and the ride would be less than an hour. Sérannes could be my husband, in my own house, and we could sleep in love and wake in love and be brought breakfast without fear. Without hiding. And I would grow fat on cake and make fatter babies and they would look like my Sérannes.

Well, perhaps not the babies. But escape seems so close. What am I to do?

Sérannes is at my father's piste, teaching. I have decided, and have entrusted my friend's girl to pack for me, as I cannot share this with even my own maid lest word fall to my father or the Count. A groom is readying my horse. If Sérannes is seen to escort me, none would think ill of it.

There must be a hundred places in the city where we can be together. A hundred-hundred. With Jean-Baptiste in the north and a house of my own, I shall come and go as I please.

I myself fetch my swords from under my bed, and bundle these in cloth, along with the Polish wheel lock pistols.

In packing I discover a forgotten trunk of things sent here from my childhood rooms and open it out of curiosity. Last year my father had gifted me, I suspect as a joke for not having a son, a tabard of the King's black. A musketeer's uniform. For whatever reason I bundle this too with the swords.

I shall just ride. Perhaps conspicuously burdened, but not overly so. I hope. It shall be just me and Lilas and an escort, as it has been a hundred times in my life. A ride south, to the pines. And once beyond that ridge, the farm road that will not meet the palace road until well north of here, and from there to the river, and home.

My heart is pounding in my chest, and I have a grand secret now, the secret of my escape.

———◖●◗———

As my friend's maid, the girl of Madame d'E_____, carries my things before me to the stables, we pass in the hall the young girl that Louis brought to my chambers that morning. She avoids me out of shame, but I note she looks ashen, drained. Whatever fate shall befall her, it is evident that it has begun to do so.

Sérannes received my message and was saddled behind the stables in a heartbeat. We ride south as we had planned before turning north to the city.

In a little wood, just before the main road, he rides up to me and kisses me. The first kiss of my free life, my true life.

I have written to Louis saying that a Madame must attend to her own house, and that I look forward to seeing him with affection at some future to-do. A little lie, but it shall buy me some distance, and some time with Sérannes.

Sérannes has taken Lilas to be boarded—this house has no stable! Something I had not enough thought of when I first arrived and am now ashamed to admit.

He has rooms here, in the city. He teaches at a salle, which while it is not as reputable as teaching at the groom's piste, holds itself well enough, or so he says. Once I am settled I would like to see it and test it, and fence again. But much to do.

Home now, for this shall be my home in Paris, and I shall remake it as I first intended. And if Louis sends for me, I will not come. I do not know what I am to do should Jean-Baptiste return.

———◦●◦———

Easy days. I arrive as late as I choose, though the household staff titter and gossip when I'm out of earshot or think I am. Amateurs. I grew up in a palace, and so can detect gossip through stone walls. In the street I am unescorted, but armed, and near-invisible in my taffeta cloak. An elegant shadow.

I have all but abandoned the remaking of my house. The livery alone is too much to contemplate, and while they dare not speak against the needed changes, each swatch and suggestion is met with a tightening of the face. They think I cannot read them. Should I begin afresh? Bring servants from the palace? Is such a thing even possible? I imagine not, besides, there are old family ties with such arrangements, generations upon generations. Some ancestress of this girl or that likely changed the diapers of my husband's grandfather. Such is the way of things. I care less by the hour.

Sérannes keeps a room above a tavern for us, and we buy discretion from the innkeeper with silver. There is always a fire in the room, and we take our fill of one another there. It is a rough place, smoke-thick and smells of mildew, but I do not care. I live for it, for our bed, for our hours, and his stories. He kisses the little pink scar across my heart. Kissing all of his scars takes me the better part of an hour. The best part.

He keeps a house in Marseilles, he tells me, on the sea, and lands there. He is practically the adopted son of an elderly Count, who sees that Sérannes is attended to. There are orange groves, and fishing boats, and mussels fresher and larger than any found at the King's table. It is always sunny, and you can lick your own skin for salt, it is so ready in the air from the sea. And all manner of people, he says. Not the parade of foreigners made up to look French, as the King dictates, but Africans, Barbary slavers and dark Catalans and the strange-accented Occitans. Turbanned Moors that sing their prayers from towers all hours of day and night. Spices and mysteries of all the world, at the end of a dock.

When he speaks of Marseilles, I can smell the blossoms on the trees.

When he kisses me, he is the ocean itself.

———— ◆ ————

Sérannes teaches a cavalry style, as though the fencer were on horseback. It is a stronger style, more forward-facing, and suited for a heavier weapon than the smallsword. I am reminded of the schiavona I was shown by one of Louis' men.

The piste is a rougher place, and these princes of the city less put-together than the grooms of the Palace. Their natural style is freer, yes, but with much reaching-over of the target. Large round scooping movements that seem to expose the forearm for too long a period, though this seems not to concern them. What seems most important to them is to clack your weapon against your opponent's blade as quickly as possible, making the bout seem more exciting than it actually is.

Such things will get one killed by anyone who knows how to take their time.

The first position mirrors that of the hanging sword. The body is upright, and perhaps more square to the opponent than I am accustomed, but only slightly. Sword-foot forward, the off hand is at the hip, inside and beneath the hilt, and the blade aligns with the lower leg, point down. You can see how this would be a down cut to protect the leg and the flank of the horse.

The guards are frozen moments. One is never to remain in such positions; only to be aware when one is entering or exiting them, to reassure oneself of one's form.

The second is a sweeping circle low and around the (imaginary) horse's head, to rest low (but not down) comfortably, aligning the blade with the bent thigh (if you were riding), sword foot forward. An all purpose ward against most attacks from the sword side, and unthreatening, as there is too much movement out of this position to attack quickly.

Stepping forward so that the off foot again is presented, the sword hand is simply extended slightly, and not elevated. The point resides in a triangle made from the line beneath the opponent's breast and the point between his eyes. In this triangle are lungs, heart, the arteries beneath the collar bone, the throat's rich vein, the face, and the eyes themselves. The sword-foot back in the third position gives you an extra step—your opponent feels out of range, when they are not.

Another step, sword foot forward (which closes the body some) the sword hand to the opposite hip, the blade extended as a shield, and the point ever in the triangle. The off hand extends to beat or even grasp the opponent's weapon. The fourth position is a fortress. There is no way in, and so is ideal for an "inferior" weapon like a dagger or a spent pistol. Or a smaller figure, such as myself. Once so entrenched, you can withstand quite the barrage, and from multiple opponents, too, until it subsides and you can take the sword foot back and rise a little into the more natural third position.

The bravos in Sérannes' salle all return predictably to the third, for they think it strikes the most heroic pose. Knowing that they will all do so makes quite a game of things, and I like to feint while they pass back into it, and when they overcompensate I lean in and pluck off their wigs with my off hand. This is always good for a laugh, and good teasing from his fellows, and Sérannes is rewarded in silver.

I love how he looks at me. No palace applause could withstand comparison to the reward and hunger of his smile.

———◄●►———

Dear God, what have we done? May God forgive my fool of a lover. There is blood everywhere. And I have been seen.

We must flee the city, and I fear for our lives.

Sérannes, you beautiful idiot. What have you done?

II

*From a letter found in the Biblioteque Nationale
attributed to Mme. Julie La Maupin.
1688—la Bastille*

There is a guard here who has heard of me.
That is something.

The fever leads to troubled sleep, and I pinch myself like a horse and feel my nose. There is no glass here so I cannot see my own eyes, but I suspect I shall not die. Not yet.

The guard is a boy, really. The others are drinking and have sent him to look after the woman, because a woman is harmless. Perhaps the men are placing bets now that I'll whip my cunny out at the young thing. They have decided no doubt that I am a whore, with all my palace-manners. But I am still a nun, or a novice anyway, and I think that is keeping me alive, and sane. In my head I am back with the sisters, the Visitandines, the Salesians.

I pray the hours: Matins when I cannot sleep, Lauds at dawn, and Prime flowing into Terce. It is usually then they send the first guard, with a bowl, and to take away night soil. Then Sext and None and Vespers, when they send the boy. I call him that though he is probably the same age as myself. Older by a year, perhaps. But a boy, still.

I could tell by his step that he was expecting a monster here, in this prison. This whore-thing spat at and ridiculed by his fellows. So, I showed him the nun. I imagine were he expecting the nun I would have played the whore, and even so, too, would there be these small kindnesses brought: candles, cleaner water. Ink and paper. A small rosary, when asked. I have requested soap, without much hope for it.

The sisters taught me to manage myself without a glass. Imagine it. I who learned to speak in front of a mirror, who spent every moment of childhood in my own reflection, home to half the mirrors in Europe, fixing my own hair without a glass, clacking a rosary in the dark.

The fever must be breaking. Each word is less a jumble here, and I realize the fever has been keeping fear at bay. I can feel the fear returning. I am in a cell, not a convent, as hard as I try to make it one. And I am here having been sentenced to death by de La Reynie, the Lieutenant General of Police, and by the King who was at my baptism and my confirmation and my wedding. The King who gave me small gifts as a child, who once gently chided us for running in the halls of the palace. The same King who now considers it right and proper that I should die for what I have done, and for what others say I have done.

Compline. *Aperi, Dómine, os meum ad benedicéndum nomen sanctum tuum: munda quoque cor meum ab ómnibus vanis, pervérsis et aliénis cogitatiónibus; intelléctum illúmina, afféctum inflámma, ut digne, atténte ac devóte hoc Offícium recitáre váleam, et exaudíri mérear ante conspéctum divínæ Majestátis tuæ.*

…that I may be heard before the Presence of Thy Divine Majesty. A prayer to God, or the King?

Before our flight:

Tempted by silver, Sérannes has agreed to witness a midnight duel behind the convent of the Carmelites. I neither know nor care as to the nature of the original grievance, but it is a show and a matter of honour, and so each opponent brings with them some sort of entourage—either newly made tavern friends or brothers by blood, there is no telling once the tide of wine has risen. There is moon enough, though the air from the river is chill and foul.

One combatant is too inebriated to fight and seems determined to attack his opponent by shoving his own skull into the other fellow's point while barking like a dog. The less-drunk fellow manages to get a few sloppily placed cuts in, most of these to the upper arm and the outer thigh, no worse than a stable-boy on a nail, really, but it enrages one party and emboldens the other. Sérannes steps in to call the exchange and declare the unwounded man the victor.

Honour sated, or what passes for honour in the duelling streets of the city.

But the uninjured is not satisfied with this; neither too are the friends of the drunkard who insist the fight has merely begun, and that their fellow's honour demands at least a chance to land a blow. Predictably this leads to shoving in the crowd, and the drawing of additional blades of varying quality. Still, horrifically dangerous, and my hand leads to my own weapon, my eyes darting. There is a pain in the back of my hands from fear, a nausea in my throat.

Instantly Sérannes draws and disarms both the combatants, pinning the obstreperous one in a soldier's hold, and yelling for the crowd to disperse before the arrival of the Maréchaussée. Duelling is of course against the dictates of the King Himself, and so each man here a traitor, should he be caught.

Reason has little power over that of crowds, and wine, and thirsty steel and bruised honour. The recently declared victor pulls a dagger and demands that Sérannes release the drunkard, so that some satisfaction may still be pursued.

Dear God. How incredibly stupid.

I have the simple and ineradicable image of Sérannes' smallsword straight through the young bravo's throat, and him there suspended, astonished.

There is a moment of total, perfect and horrible stillness.

Madness, with some of the wiser and more sober scrambling to leave the scene, while others lunging at the opposing sides, or those next to them, their blood up. One well-dressed idiot, who had hitherto contained himself, draws and turns, lunging towards me, and not inexpertly.

I draw and disarm him on reflex, thinking that would be the last of it. My thoughts are of Sérannes and the imminently-arriving marshals. But my disarmed gentleman, now insulted, comes at me unarmed.

Presumably he thought my sex superseded the fact that I had a drawn weapon pointed at him, and that I obviously knew how to use it given that his own sword was a good few paces away in the gutter. Regardless, he comes at me in a rage, and while I do not wish to kill the poor fellow, I crack him across the jaw with my sword hilt.

I had not thought of the quillons. Small, ancillary things. Leftovers from the great cross-hilts of longswords, once hands-long but now the length of an index finger. But still steel and sharp and moving quickly. In this case, moving quickly across the soft pad of flesh beneath the jawbone, and removing it completely.

He chokes and falls, the bottom of his tongue already falling out of the purse-like opening in his throat.

I freeze, not in horror but in fascination. Even in the torchlight, I can make out the anatomy I had only seen in my father's books on physic. Here are the strings which give men voice, hold them together, give them life. And here they are, cut. I should feel revulsion, but it is so beautiful. So perfect, the musculature and tissue and ligament. A concert of structures. My hand is at my own throat, probing and feeling for these same instruments within.

A man in that crowd, his shoulders breaking through the sea of it like the prow of a ship. I know the face, with its peculiar broken nose. Staring at me. I am his destination now.

My arrest is to be my death.

Sérannes grabs my arm roughly and hauls me to an alley across the street from the convent. Escape, though my mind is still unspooling these events. The man I've killed. The man intent on killing me, or at least seeing me dead.

And so to home, to a second hastily packed escape in as many months. To fetch Lilas and leave notes for the servants and bundle cheese and meat and bread and wine and cakes, my taffeta cloak and boy's breeches and my warm black musketeer's tabard, sword and pistols. Only one wig-box, a nightdress, a morning dress, and a pale blue gown I can get into myself. All stuffed into saddle bags, and insisting despite protest from Jean-Baptiste's maid (my maid, I suppose) that I carry them myself.

In the doorway, before the stairs and a waiting lover and my sweet Lilas in the street below, I note that there is not a drop of blood on me.

——◄●►——

Not a drop of blood on me. Absurd, now, that my night dress is such a massacre. And I do not know if the tavern-girl has the sense to wash it in salt. If not, the linens are fine enough to pay for our nights here, and we can hold on to each precious sous that must last us to the end of our road, Sérannes' fine houses in Marseilles.

The girl here is I think simple, until I asked her for blood-cloths. Four days on horseback, first west toward the sea and then south, well clear of the Palace, and beyond. Four days and scarcely a hundred miles from Versailles.

I am in no condition to ride, blood-cloths or no, with the moon vexing me. At least this means I am not with child, and we have Sérannes' little sheep-skin friend to thank for that.

God, to have forgotten tooth-powder. They have none here. My mouth tastes of road dust. My mother always swore by a powder of ground cuttlefish and sugar, which I insisted must be pink or blue. There is nothing here but birch twigs, which make my gums bleed.

Ugh, what chance is there that Sérannes can bring back some chocolate? Dare I hope?

I am beyond hope. I shall die in this filthy tavern-bed, bled to my grave by my courses, with bad breath and a bruised thigh. Chocolate-less.

Everything aches and there is a glowing purple rose on my inner thigh—and not from love, but from that damned saddle. I shall use whatever livres we've escaped with to buy a man's saddle, and on the next leg of our journey I shall wear breaches and ride astride. My backside and my spine cannot take any more sidesaddle. And yet upon reaching this decision comes my monthly blood, the cramps buried beneath the general ache of riding for days.

It is weeks to Marseille and I mean to arrive in some better condition than the miserable creature which now lies a-bed, in mold-scented sheets and the reek of piss and dried sick on the floorboards. Blood too, there, by the door, red into the wood from how many years ago none could tell. Childbirth or murder or more likely a tavern-brawl from downstairs, with a bleeding drunkard staggering into the room for a final night's sleep, making it perhaps a full step towards the bed before falling to his fate.

Tavern rooms are written of such stories as their stains. I pluck a flea from my neck.

—◖●◗—

Three hundred miles to Marseilles, Sérannes tells me. Two weeks, at this pace. To our life together, finally. Is this our life? Rough-sleeping in the wood off the road, only to ride all day in hopes of finding a tavern by nightfall?

The road is not a quiet place. To feed the ravenous creature of the Palace, a constant parade trudges through the ruts to bring silk, sea-fruits, pineapples, tradesmen, silver and glass, all from the great ports of France and all along this road to Versailles like an obscene digestive tract. The Palace devouring all of France, hour by hour. We travel some one hundred and eighty miles, by the reckoning of the stones here, the descendants of Roman stones—farther than most will travel in a lifetime—and still we find ourselves in the shadow of the shining monster.

South, then.

The day it rained, we made good time. Fifty miles, with the third horse. A hard ride, but at least we were out of it sooner. The next day we walked the horses after a good brushing, and I saw to their shoes. We will need a farrier upon our arrival, but they should hold until then.

I dream of the Palace, that I had awoken between my mother and father as I would often as a little girl. I was about to tell my mother that I was cold, that my hips were sore, when I woke to dawn in the forest, a tree root digging into my back. But my head is on Sérannes' sleeping chest. I pull his cloak tighter around us both, and I place my hand over his heart.

I love the perfection of such moments, even though they are unplanned. Though I must confess a certain weariness to riding, to sleeping on tree-roots, to ask for an inn of travelers heading north, only to find that we have just passed one off some forest road, and to trudge to the next.

Sérannes is recognized by a merchant, a friendly fellow, and so we are assured that no word of our misadventure has reached this far south. And I am introduced merely as "Julie" so it is clear that our relationship warranted no further inquiry. He brings us a meal, saving our precious remaining silver, and much wine. The merchant (whose name I don't recall even hearing) brags about being the friend of such an esteemed swordsman, which sets the locals to bristling. He doesn't look so great, come the comments from the tavern. I cringe from the stupidity of it, and Sérannes is not so quick to return to the disaster outside the Carmelites. So he does something curious, as means of deflection. He challenges the boys there to challenge me.

Laughter, then silence. Then more laughter still.

Wagers slapped heartily on tables, cups drained, and to much cheer we go outside to a hastily poured piste of sawdust, just barely under the rafters of the place. There is a bit of wind.

The first is overconfident, and I remain in fourth position and parry, and parry, and parry to frustrate him. When he becomes careless I cheekily slap his sword-hand away with my off-hand, but still I do not press an attack. His footwork is terrible, and so on his lunge I merely place the fort of my blade over his tip, driving it into the dirt. I take a long step, clap a hand on his shoulder, and give him a peck on the cheek. This sets the place to laughter, my opponent too laughs in embarrassment and seeks another kiss, which I grant.

The next boy is nervous, and stiff. Jerky little reaches of sentiment, which I evade almost lazily. I can see him boiling over, goaded by his friends, until he charges me. I simply step aside and let him pass, whipping his buttocks with the flat of my sword. The laughter is sweet as applause, and I take a modest bow.

He turns, and takes several good, committed lunges, which I must focus to parry. He is wiry, but strong. Ill-trained though, as he knows only one attack, and that repeated, and predictable. I assume a high fifth guard, protecting the top of my head—just for drama's sake, he is lunging over and over toward my heart—and shoot the blade down sharply allowing me well inside his guard, my shoulder into his chest. With my off-hand, I merely remove his sword from his grip, and pivot my blade so it rests high and inside, between his legs.

His eyes flare in anger, but he has two friends who wisely grab his shoulders so he could go neither forward nor back, and thus preventing him from gelding himself. The two pound him on the back and offer to buy him another drink, while all applaud, and the sawdust rains with silver.

It's a boy! cries one from the back, in disbelief that a girl could best two men so.

A boy? I cry back. A boy?

Still holding my sword in my right hand, my left undoes my chemise and I bare my breasts. I hold my shirt open with both hands, still gripping my blade in my right, and turn a full slow circle.

I am no boy! I shout. I am La Maupin! and then the tavern shakes, without and within, with applause and thunder and approval. Those who withheld their silver previously do not do so now, and the coins catch and tumble the light of the torches back into the night sky.

So I sing. *L'incoronazione di Poppea*, Monteverdi. Just a part. But they have never heard such a thing, not from a bare-breasted girl, armed with a sword atop a pile of silver. It is magic, and it is my gift to them.

The tavern-keeper seems well-pleased, as each man stays to recount what they had seen with yet another cup of wine to sustain their voices. And

Sérannes and I retire upstairs. He is particularly ferocious and attentive.

A bed and a fire! Even a warm basin to wash my feet. Simple luxuries, although I'm sure the populace of Palace daughters would find my state beneath that of their maids' sisters. I am sore. But undeniably happy.

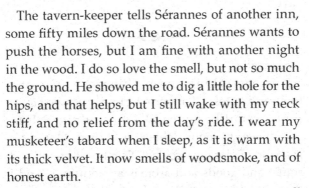

The tavern-keeper tells Sérannes of another inn, some fifty miles down the road. Sérannes wants to push the horses, but I am fine with another night in the wood. I do so love the smell, but not so much the ground. He showed me to dig a little hole for the hips, and that helps, but I still wake with my neck stiff, and no relief from the day's ride. I wear my musketeer's tabard when I sleep, as it is warm with its thick velvet. It now smells of woodsmoke, and of honest earth.

So we have stopped early afternoon, Sérannes all day counting the silver from last night. I tell him it is strange. We have enough to get to Marseilles. What does it matter, a few sous or several? Once we arrive he has a grand house, he told me. And we need so little. A bed, clean water. Oranges. And there are spices too I've never tasted, and am eager to. But the money seems to matter to Sérannes for reasons I cannot fathom.

Tethering the horses, we fetch powder and ball for my pistols—iron pyrite, too, as flint will wear down the wheel. Sérannes teaches me to shoot. Once you are over the fear of the crack, and the kick, it is not so different from a sword thrust, or reining a horse. It wishes to go one way, you wish it to go another, and it must be made to obey through strength and will. They are heavy, my pistols, but to crack a tree at such a distance and with such accuracy, surely such a thing is magic, though a dark one.

Again to the road. There is only the road. But I can sense a change in the air, a sweetness of blossom and fruit. And eventually, finally, the scent of the sea.

Marseilles.

It is everything and nothing. A music of a thousand notes, all at once. I can discern no single tune. So unlike my childhood, and the Palace, where everything is deliberate, crafted. Marseilles is a kind of glorious accident. People and sound and traffic and goods and aromas all colliding. And I think I have never truly had coffee before now.

We are at an inn, Le Logis de Panier, Sérannes and I, just north of the city. We bathe to wash the road from us, and in the water here the girl put orange blossoms, and cinnamon. I smell something like a cake, I think, but it is better than the fog of my own sweat, and that of Lilas.

Sérannes wishes the day to make himself presentable to his Master, and promises that after that we will go to his house, by the sea. He says it is a villa, like the Italians have, the roofs terracotta like Spaniards with arches like Moors. In the meantime I have put on my blue silk gown, and a few simple jewels. He says this while attending to our wigs, as he has a hand for such things, and they became a bit mashed during our journey.

—◖●◗—

A dock at morning, with ships arriving from all the world. Barrels of ice and salt, peppers and strange fruits from Africa, and men with them. I cannot stop myself from staring at so many beautiful hands, the storied hands of working men. So many Moors here, with their speech like music, and the songs of their priests from towers. And despite the crowds, there is a sweet smell to the people, washed clean by the sea air. By contrast, Versailles is a pot with a lid, and all those inside merely stewing.

Sérannes very sweetly buys me a monkey. A wee little thing, honey brown, but clearly unwell. Bleary eyes and patchy fur. He hops on my shoulder and strokes my face, the hands of a tiny old man. He chits in my ear and kisses my cheek, and then leaps away into the market. I laugh, but Sérannes swears, cheated. I do not mind so much.

Everything here is a riot of life and pleasure.

—◖●◗—

Tonight, I wished to see the opera here, but Sérannes insists there is none. I find the idea impossible. Surely this far south we are even closer to Italians?

Today Sérannes returns from seeing his Master, but he will not discuss it. He seems upset and speaks sharply to me. I can tell he's been drinking, and he wants me to change into riding clothes. Breeches and tabard, and that I should be armed. I tell him I was sick of road-clothes and can think of no reason to go out in a sword in such a city as this. The warmth, I think, makes everyone sleepy and kind, and all things move slower here. Content. But he is insistent, and he calls for a carriage. We find ourselves at a tavern hall back up the road, dressed as we have been for the last weeks.

It is a game, I think, as lovers play. But there are other, newer games to play here in Marseilles, and I want to see them. Despite that we are inside a carriage, the road makes me instantly weary, and on our arrival, he calls for a chicken and a pitcher of wine, neither of which are good, and both he dispatches over-quickly. I had never seen him so vulgar, and he is even unkind to the tavern-girl.

My gallant gone, replaced by this ill-tempered lout, spilling wine and shouting at girls. I think to tease him out of his mood and mockingly demand that he apologize to the girl, as a gentleman. I beckon her over, and she is frightened. I have seen the look of girls frightened by men before, though such a countenance has never visited my face.

His means of apology is to grab her about the waist, forcing her onto his lap, and mash an unwanted kiss. To offend me or inspire jealousy by way of upbraiding me. I raise an eyebrow, as I do when I am very angry.

Come here, I reach out to the girl gently. Sit.

She seems grateful for an invitation away from Sérannes, though she is clearly used to such treatment, and expected worse. She comes and sits on my lap, and I brush the hair from her face with my fingers.

Kiss me, I say, and the men at the table pound their fists into the wood in approval, daring her.

Or not, I tell her. It's up to you.

But there is some fire in her, and this is no timid peck, but a lurid thing, an animal thing. My pulse rises in my throat unbidden, and it drowns out the raucous shouts of the men. After, she smiles at me and nods, collecting the coppers newly spilled on the table for her show.

Sérannes stews on the other side of the table, grease from the chicken on his chin.

You're going to perform for these men? he says. His voice is unkind. Sing, then! and I cannot tell if he is attempting to be cruel or wishing to change the tone of the evening by way of apology.

But I do sing, and it quiets the place, and there is applause of a nature more boisterous than I am used to. Instruments appeared from under tables and from within packs, and there is a bright pepper to the music. A few sous in a pile before Sérannes grows to a few more, and wine is pressed into my hand, and the tavern-girl even returns for another kiss. One of the musicians puts his hand on my thigh, but I throw him a look which shrivels his resolve if not his manhood.

I am not so much tired as bored, but Sérannes wants me to keep singing. One more song became another song, and then I gather my things and venture outside, where there is more than one carriage for hire.

You're taking that carriage? Sérannes challenges. How will you pay for it?

I'll walk if I have to, I say.

But he grabs me and kisses me, and I would knee him then and there if he didn't smell so good. If I were not in love with him.

I should kill you in your sleep, you know, I say.

So long as you sleep with me, he says, then I shall die a happy man.

Which makes me laugh. We take the carriage here, back to Paniers. But the wine takes him, and he is snoring now.

I do not mind the singing, even singing for money. I love it, to be honest, and the silver is a kind of scorekeeping. But I cannot understand the need for it, if we are to see Sérannes' house tomorrow. All our counting coins was to bring us here, and now we have arrived I see no need of them.

One of my pistols is gone.

Fuming.
Sérannes is gone.

I awake to find him gone, and I spend the morning discovering a coffee house, just off the quay. It is beautiful (how I have missed actual painted ceilings!) and serves fresh mussels, and potatoes from the New World sliced hot in olive oil. I would love it here, but my temper is still up.

I return to our inn to find Sérannes here and ask him if we are leaving today to his house.

Impossible, he says.

I do not understand. How can a man not return to his own house? He had seen to his Master, or so he tells me. He is packing, and I do not know where we are going.

He sold the pistol, he admits, after some interrogation.

I ask him why he would do such a thing, and he says he needs the money. A scant few livres for the thing, when it was worth a hundred times more! He says I knew nothing of such things. I insist it was mine, and he asks me how I came to possess it. I am furious.

He commands that I be silent, or else return to my father, or the Count, or my husband. How dare he speak to me that way? I gave him everything, left and risked everything for him. Because I loved him.

Do love him.

I want to strike him but think better of it. He would strike me back, and I would have to kill him. Here, in this room which felt like respite, but now I see for him it feels like exile. He is penniless, landless. And I have fallen for a lie.

He has gone.

There are plentiful candles here, each with their price inscribed into the wax. I have lit them all. Despite the hour, I have called for a bath to be drawn up.

The innkeeper has a son, perhaps eight, who reminds me somewhat of the monkey from the market—honey-coloured hair, yet tired and unwell. Patchy. He rouses me from hours of tears to tell me there is trouble in the square nearby. That I am to come at once.

Sérannes.

I find him outside an alehouse, like the English have. And it is with Englishmen that he quarrels drunkenly. So that is what has become of the money from my pistol.

He has his sword in hand, as have about seven others, who goad him in ghastly-accented French, and shout insults I do not understand. Seeing him I think, these are all dead men. They are shouting from their grave.

I am in my blue gown, with my black cloak and smallsword, and they take no notice of me. Sérannes sees me but offers no sign of recognition. Is he trying to save me, by ignoring me?

They make for him clumsily, three at once. This makes things easier for him as he can always keep one of them in the other's way, and line them up as he chooses.

I cannot see his movements, but I watch them fall, two, then the third, as the others fill in the space left by their fellows. A flurry of blows, and Sérannes staggers.

I cry out. Three standing calculate how I have betrayed my presence, and its significance. They run to me across the small, ancient square, leaving one to Sérannes.

I see their faces in the torchlight. Hungry, confused, driven by something I seem to have no part of, and yet play a part in.

I drive the first one clean through the heart, draw my pistol and shoot the next in the chest, not three paces away. The pistol's crack serves to swing Sérannes' opponent's head around, and Sérannes' sword finds its home under the man's ribs.

Five more would-be assailants pour out of the alehouse, brandishing staves and pokers, whatever weapons are to be found.

Run! I shout.

Run.

Resigned, Sérannes flies into the alley across the square, leaving me in the street with some six men.

The one who had seen me drop his two friends stretches out his arms, pushing the small crowd back inside. Fear of another pistol, I imagine. A rare act of common sense. By the time he looks back at me, I am swallowed by black taffeta, and shadow. I return to the inn, my hands shaking and reeking of spent powder. Brimstone.

The boy here is nowhere to be seen, but the innkeeper's wife pours another copper bucket of scalding water into the tub.

I should weep, but I cannot. There is only enough crying any woman can be expected to do in a single day.

Last season at Versailles we were visited by some grand emissary of the Emperor of China. They arrived with a vast retinue, and there was a buzz of silks and competition among those re-gifted with their shimmering bolts. Some imperial dressmaker was among the entourage and had fitted some of the more important ladies in traditional (one expects) attire. To these, though, the King insisted upon French embellishment, no doubt to the horror of the dressmaker in question.

But it was gorgeous and shimmering, and all the chinoiserie had been dragged from attics and storerooms and dressed the halls. But after the ball and the reception and the vaguely scandalous after-party, where Elise and I had taken too much wine, we set out to the gardens to watch the sun come up, despite the drizzle of rain. And what had been a magic of glittering candles in red paper lanterns was now a sad parade of melting, bleeding crepe, staining the marble in spent misery.

I am such a thing as these. A spent lantern, collapsed and staining the stairs in the rain.

I was wrong, I think, about Marseilles. This riot of colour, the carelessness and casualty of everything, every person. It is not freedom, just ignorance. No one has taught these people how to dress, how to behave. The Moors do—they have a deliberation to every gesture, a planned quality to their movements and transactions, but it is unfathomable to me. There is a laziness to the others, which was once appealing but now just seems to me untidy.

Truly I do miss the Palace. All the meticulous care gone into every gilt and cut-glass surface, all marble and porcelain and flawlessness that takes endless effort to establish and maintain. My heart is a riot and I do not wish it so. I wish for the cool of marble pillars in the shade. The ticking crispness of footsteps in the Palace hallways. Here there is only the crunch of gravel, or the sandy scratch of flagstones.

Sérannes said it to be hurtful, but should I go back? To Jean-Baptiste? To Louis? To my father? Is there nothing for me but to be in the shadow of one man or another?

The men here see me, they see Versailles in the way I move, or the way I refrain from movement. And they approach sniffing like dogs. The dockworkers and sailors are at least honest and bear the scent of the sea, but the gentlemen of Marseilles are just pretending, and badly. Like circus bears in brocade.

Oh I wish I could sing here. But there is no opera. Do I take Lilas (I have checked on her, and she is well-boarded, I have livres enough of my own to see to that) and go to Italy? A woman alone on the road. Is such a thing possible? Sérannes had road-goods; a tinderbox and ironware. Canvas, hatchet, and a salt-box. I have nothing—one cannot chop wood with a smallsword. I could book passage, perhaps, and sail to Paris. But what of poor Lilas?

Of all the goods from all the world, Marseilles draws in coffee like a breath of air.

I have seen the black sheen of the beans drying in the sun on the quay. Barrels of cherries you can slice open with your thumb and see the green seed there, before drying and carted to the roasters, blazing heat onto the street in waves even on a scalding day. And here to this café, where I sit and watch the steam rise from my cup and try not to think too much.

There are musicians who come in here, clearly they are students or the sons of good families, who do not play from ambition but enjoyment. Little songs, enjoyed for sport, and not the more complex pieces learned and mastered by those seeking employment.

One of the musicians is very flirtatious and, discovering that I am from Versailles, asks about his cousin, who by shocking coincidence is my notorious friend Elise.

At this they all sit down with me, and we have cakes and coffee together. I apologize for looking a fright, but they are all fascinated that I had taken to the road without carriage. I confess my story of running away with my lover, and it gives them something to talk about for a year, I swear. Marc (Elise's cousin) insists we write a letter to her then and there, together, wishing he could see the look on her face. I suggest she has already concocted a superior story of her own, and was dining on it, and he laughs agreeing. Nevertheless, we take turns writing the letter.

They all ask where I was staying in Marseilles, and I tell them of the little inn in Paniers, to their horror. Marc points through the window across the street, to show me high arched windows above. A new building, one of the few fashionable edifices in the city (is Marseilles a city? It is no Paris. A town? I shall ask). Anyway, there are apartments there to be rented, and no one in them. My new friends encourage me to establish myself there and host a salon.

And a piste, I say jokingly.

They are riveted. They ask where I had learned such an art, and had I been in many duels. A Palace-daughter teaching swordplay in the south! This delights them, and I spy a path to turning their delight in my favour.

I confess that I did not bring with me the livres for such an undertaking, and Marc insists on loaning me money until such time as I could have funds sent from Paris. Of course I refuse, of course he persists, and of course I relent with reserved gratitude.

Marc also presses upon me that he would ask his sister, Lisette, to loan me a girl, that I might have someone to attend me. The rest chime in as to which merchants to see for Parisian fashion—shoes and wigs and furnishings, that the salon of their desire take shape. Another tells me of a stable nearby that would serve as a piste, discreetly, were I to offer instruction. This latter somewhat in jest I think.

But I shall show them.

Busy. So very busy.

I ensconce myself in the apartments across from the café. Little here now but bed and desk until everything arrives, but tall ceilings and silk wallpaper in pale blue. Not the Palace style of my friends' imagining, but the younger, brighter style from Italy. No heroes in rain-darkened marble, but cherubs in simple white plaster. My salon is to be spring, and joyous.

I find myself in great need of joy.

Marc arranges it so that the best gentlemen of the city (it is, indeed, a city, so they insist) help fund the salon, and they are amused by the style I have chosen. But there is not room in my heart to care for this otherwise marvelous news.

Lisette fills me to overflowing. I am overripe fruit in the sun, warmed and succulent and bursting. And it is Lisette who tastes me.

She never sleeps, and exists only on sugar—and this never brown. Only the dyed sugars in the pinks and yellows and blues I have always loved, which is everywhere here, and on this she thrives like a hummingbird. The only word she speaks is "yes." I adore her.

We met in the café and I was charmed at once. She is so doll-like, so delicate, with a long throat teased by soft golden hair. A kind of blond I've never seen, and I cannot resist playing with it, curling it with my fingers. She took to my lap like a kitten at first sight, and she laughs at everything.

We dine at her mother's house, with Marc and his musician friends, and we play cards until the servants yawn. And while the boys make their past-midnight advances and innuendo, Lisette asks me to read her to sleep. So, hand in hand we climb the stairs to her chamber, and into her grand, cool bed (they do not warm the beds here), and I read her Greek until she pretends to sleep, smiling. And then I play with her hair, and breathe in her skin.

It is not a wicked thing to do, for girls to lie with one another. Not here, and not in the Palace, but I know the black crows of the King's wife speak evil of it, and in all other places such love is scandalized.

As a younger girl I know several of my friends who would play at romance, practicing kisses and pretending pleasures, great long love letters with no one to send them to but those whom they knew, whom they could trust. And that meant sisters of friends and maids, who were always grateful for small love-tokens or a night in better sheets. It is just an innocence. And for some, never spoken of but of course always spoken of, they remain in their inclinations, taking only other women to their beds. Such women are needed for the stories of men, I always thought, but it is not so.

When I kiss Lisette, I am as big as all the world.

The new apartments are a garden indoors. This is how I had wished to make Jean-Baptiste's home in Paris, those months ago, but here is my dream realized. There are even rabbits, wild and nervous things, and they scratch the wallpaper, but still they are beautiful and soft, when you can catch them, trembling on your lap. But the sun makes them drowsy, and agreeable.

Lisette and I bathe every day, as is the custom here. It is the only way to preserve the skin in the heat, without getting rashes. Likewise we remove all the hair from our bodies with razors, like the Moorish women. Otherwise the skin rises, red and angry. So we bathe in cool water, with flowers, and wear loose shifts of linen or cotton from New France, or we lounge in each other's nakedness, reading and planning parties.

Lisette has an aptitude for such things. For the guests each sense must be addressed. The scent of flowers. Colour wherever the eye should go. Music. Texture in the table-cloths and upholstery and the weight of spoons. And of course flavour. I have brought with me a lifetime of such parties, and merely need to recall one or another, and our guests are fascinated and insisting we do whichever theme or dish that I mention. And for this they are generous, and Lisette and I are magnificent together.

Alas she has no interest in swordplay, and merely laughs when I suggest she learn. Should I scold her on this, she but kisses me, and that is the afternoon gone. We wear nothing but light, and the scent of one another.

———⟨●⟩———

I awake to her kissing me, and her hair falls over her face making a private world just for the two of us. A blond cave of her face, her mouth, the morning light shining through a sheet of gold.

I would stay in such a world forever.

———⟨●⟩———

There is indeed an agreeable stable here to serve as a piste, and a salle of sorts. I am a poorly-kept secret, as are all good secrets, and the young bravos of the port—screened by Marc, of course—pay well for the curiosity of being instructed in the art by a woman.

Such beautiful swords, and never before drawn, so many of them. I teach them to care for the blades, to avoid fingerprints, of how to oil and sharpen them. They scoff, as they have servants for such things, but I tell them as my father told me, that to understand the sword you must care for it like a living thing. Like a horse. Of course they have never cared for a horse either, but there is only so much I can be expected to teach them.

For many their form is quite good, and they favour the Spanish style. Some are even versed in Moorish forms, using their curved blades in great slashes, which, while majestic, is useless with a smallsword. One can hardly go about town armed with a scimitar as though one were on the way to a beheading.

But every day the measure, the guard, imbrocatta stocatta mandritti roversi. And again.

One fellow arrives drunk and belligerent, so I insist he leave. He says he will not suffer the commands of a woman, and I ask him what he was doing in my piste then. He calls me a circus monkey, so I bid him draw his blade.

Slow, idiot creature.

I draw and slash him across the back of his wrist before he can get his sword out. There is perhaps more than a little blood, and his whole hand crimson, dripping into the sawdust. His friends accompany him home, apologizing, fearing that I might banish them from my instruction.

Lisette has decided we need our own staff for the salon so we must hire some, but I find such things tedious. Yet she has no experience in these matters, and I have no one to defer to. I have asked her to wait until a solution presents itself.

I never imagined meeting someone more impatient than myself. She is utterly marvelous.

Marc tells me that the drunkard I reprimanded the other day is dead.

It was no killing injury, but he did not tend the wound, and returned to drinking. The filth of the horses got into the cut, somehow, and between the blood-loss and the fever he shook himself in his sleep and choked on his own tongue.

This is the fourth man I have killed, but I feel no sin for it. Though it was my sword that scratched him, it was his ill manner and lack of sense which felled him. Break the skin around rust and horses, you must wash the wound and salve it, or stitch it if needed. Some cannot bear the stitching, but I imagine it is less uncomfortable than choking to death on parts of your own person. He died of stupidity, and that is the entirety of the matter.

We have a party to plan for. A Moorish harem! The gentlemen will all be in turbans, and we have been inventing a dance. There are ladders all over the salon hanging fabrics from the ceiling, and a parade of cushion-vendors and carpet sellers. I found a snake charmer, but Lisette will not let the creature in the apartments. I think it is the first time she ever said no to me.

I gifted her a curio from the market: a carving in some exotic wood, in shape entirely obscene. She laughed her fairy-laugh at this, and kissed it, and laughed some more.

———◦●◦———

They have taken her.

I shall slit their throats when I am no longer shaking with rage or crying.

When I find out where they have taken her.

Apparently the family of the drunkard circulated a letter among some of the families here, saying that I was "a corruption." Because I dared scratch the hand of one of their beloved sons, and he too dimwitted to attend to it. And because I dared love a girl, and that desperately. They will attend our parties and drink and flirt and applaud our dancing; they will learn to thrust and parry and riposte in the styles novel to them—but they will turn and bite the very hand that offers them art and learning and culture.

At dawn, two armed men force their way into the apartment, shoving Lisette's maid to the floor and bursting into our room. We awake, startled, and one grabs Lisette by the hair, close to the scalp, and hauls her naked from our bed. She is sobbing and screaming, and I reach under the bed for the pistol, but remember of course it is not loaded. Still naked, I leap upon him, screaming, and he bashes my face with a gauntlet. He calls me whore, slattern. Monster.

His accomplice stands with a drawn sword, aiming it at me. I refuse to cover myself, and stand naked and spitting and insulting him. The first drags Lisette writhing and howling like an animal, while I curse at his fellow, coward that he is, facing a naked woman with a weapon.

I follow them both to the foyer, where waits Lisette's father. The second man re-enters our chamber to fetch a sheet, and they bundle her up like a moth in a spider's web, and haul her to the street. Her father appraises my nakedness and sneers. I spit at him too.

I will kill him. He and his thugs. I will slaughter them all.

I have been trying to see her, having been repeatedly turned away, and my messengers likewise refused.

I write to Elise for details as to where else she might have been sent. A country estate? Does the family keep houses in Paris?

I must find her. She is my light.

How can I sleep? Our bed still carries the scent of her, her perfume on my hands.

She is my light.

They return my letters to her. I send them by the hour, and the house returns them just as quickly.

I write to Marc. I pace between the café and the apartment to see if he or a reply appears at either.

The devil approaches the table at the café as though I had been expecting him. Perhaps I have. He is no longer the worst thing in the world, at least in this moment.

The spider de La Reynie pulls away the chair and sits, a fluid motion, beckoning for coffee without taking his cold eyes off me. I don't even bother looking for the men outside, I can feel them there. Nor do I ask him what he is doing in Marseilles, or how he found me. The answer is simply that he is able to do so.

The end of your misadventure, it seems, he says.

I say nothing.

Will you be returning to Paris? he says.

There are some men I'd like to kill first, I tell him.

That, he says, does not seem beyond your talents.

You among them, I say.

Ah, he replies. On that we must part company. Of course, there are other men to kill. It might take your mind off things. He wipes a trace of sugar from his moustache.

Where is she? I demand.

Your paramour? I have no idea. Honestly, he assures me.

I actually believe him.

It still strikes me as absurd, that here is a man whose imperium, the power of who lives and dies, may rival the King himself. And here he wishes me to be a pawn on his board.

But I am no pawn. I am a queen. I am not armed, and there is no knife on the table, but I could make use of this bottle and at least crack his skull open before his men could burst in and shoot me.

He watches me consider this, understanding.

And wordlessly, he rises and leaves.

Marc finally breaks with his cowardice and tells me where she is.

The convent, he says.

Which? I ask. There must be a thousand convents. A thousand thousand.

The Visitandines, he tells me. The Salesians. In Avignon. Some sixty miles to the north.

I ask if she had sent any word for me, but she has not. She has been watched constantly, he says, and she is forbidden to write. Only to pray.

Very well then. Pray, my love. Pray for me.

I am coming.

It is late, and I have lit a small fire. I wonder if they can see it, the flames in the woods, from the convent.

Do they look out from those narrow windows, searching for lights at dusk?

I could not do the journey in one day, and not even two.

I left everything. There are no servants, but I suspect Marc will inquire soon enough, and see to the rent until I return, if ever.

I packed for the road, as Sérannes had taught me to do. Breeches and tabard, sword and pistol. I told no one where I was going, or even that I was going. I stopped a boy at the market and bade him bring me road-goods; these heavier than I imagined. I did not bring Lilas, as I had no idea where to stable him once I arrived. I have never seen a nun on a horse. So I bought a small dapple, thinking he would be quick, but he had his own pace and would not be hastened. Last night at an inn, but no song, and no questions. I supped in my room, and slept fitfully 'til dawn.

I am hungry, but that is just as well. I am cold, but this too I imagine I will need to get used to. This night, in sight of my Lisette's prison, shall be my penance.

In the morning I shall bury my goods and set loose this horse. I will fashion a cloak from the blanket with a simple pin, and go barefoot along the pilgrim's road to the Visitandines in only my nightdress. That will be my part, the simple, pious girl who never kissed my father's master, never took to his bed, never cut the life out of a man or had the same spilled within me. That never loved or laid or longed for the girl behind those stone walls I can barely make out in the falling light.

I am to become again the pliant girl of Mass, palms open, tongue presented softly for the body of God.

The sisters here have nothing—can have nothing—even to the point where our habits and small crucifixes are confiscated regularly and exchanged. Nothing is "ours", not even the statuary in the chapel. These are replaced when the priest comes for Mass.

I take the black of a choir sister—out of pride, I suppose, a sin for which I have dutifully confessed. Lisette has taken the white habit of a lay sister, tasked with domestic duties.

It is more comfortable than I expected. A proper bed, for one, and clean. The food is good, if simple, and the hours not onerous. We do not keep Matins nor Lauds, so we are at liberty to sleep from perhaps ten o'clock until breakfast, after Prime. When the bells ring, we are to "run to the spouse"—we cease all labour or conversation or even private prayer and return to the chapel.

Still, there is a chill to the ancient walls of the monastery, and the discipline of silence, and chores. I tend to the horses, and I regret loosing the dapple before I entered here, as I did not think they would have a stable for him. Regardless, the stables here were not well organized, and I set things to right, with fresh straw and clean water, brushing the tack clean of rust, and oil the leather. There is an older mare here, kept for pity, and I mix her a salve of leopard's bane to ease the obvious pain in her hips.

It was some days before I could enter properly and stayed in the pilgrims' hut away from the sisters until my confession could be heard, and then a week again until Mass, after which I could take my vows.

They cut my hair. I did not think this a crime until I was shorn of it. But Lisette gasped when she saw it, chopped like a boy. Her hair too, the beautiful golden cave in which I would kiss her mouth, now gone. Although this does bare the line from her collar bone to her throat, and this awakens something in me. To little avail, for here there is no time for love, and no place for it. Stolen conversations. We feign no previous recognition. They call me Emilie, my middle name.

There are children here. This came as a shock to me. But some of the sisters are widowed, and for the year they spend at the monastery, their small children are in attendance. They are sweet and semi-wild things who mostly stick to the garden and are shooshed out of the kitchens, and not unkindly.

So once more for me a life of girls, of singing and Mass, and of horses. I have undone the world of men by crossing this threshold. And as desperate as I am for Lisette, the rhythm of my life here is a balm. "A daughter from the heart of Christ", in humility and gentleness, and in this I have found perhaps some measure of forgiveness. But I do not know.

This is just a role I play. And while I am already sentimental for it, I can feel it skittering over the surface of my heart, never penetrating. Like fencing with batons—yes, this thrust would be true, but we are practicing, pretending. There is no bite to the blade.

The bells! The tide of the day turns, and I run to sing to it.

It is a kind of dream here, which I suppose is the point. It is not the world. Oh, it is, when there are little hurts, when the children are cross or there is a scraped knee or a dropped plate. But we go in a kind of fog from sleep to prayer to breakfast to chores to prayer, and for each there is a song, which I find myself singing without ever really waking up.

There is a sister here, Patrice, who looks at me with scorn. She can see whatever stain of sin in me I myself do not feel. Her loathing gives her power, but not over me. Perhaps over some ghost of her own. I ignore her. I ignore everything. This is what we do, we who come here, ignore everything but the voice of God in our heads. I have taken another husband in God, my own husband abandoned by a lie of omission, and another layer of vows.

Lisette, in her habit, is just a dream-figure. I can walk past her in the hall, or in the gardens, and barely recognize her, feeling nothing. But in the evening, I remember her, and a fire is lit, and my mouth goes dry. I wish to dream of our apartments in Marseilles, with our rabbits and our bed, and waking up to her skin, her kiss on my bare hip.

But I have not been granted such a dream.

Months, now. The soil feels different to step on. More brittle. Does the earth itself age, year after year? If so, my steps age the earth, wearing steps into dust.

Lisette leaves our stolen hour, and I dare light a candle, though every creak and tick of this ancient place brings the panic of discovery.

I am deliriously happy.

By moonlight, Lisette finds her way to my room. I can no longer think of it as a cell. She climbs into my bed, her feet freezing. But I do not care. She is mine, again, at last, mine. My chest roars with blood again, and I ache for her again, and I am myself, alive, again.

I have been sleepwalking, and she has awoken me. I would beg her forgiveness for allowing myself to fall into this distance, this discipline. But I do not beg. I simply lack the talent.

The scent of her is on my hands, and sated, I shall sleep.

I have a plan.

The hall and chapel of our monastery were once, many centuries ago, built in solitude, parallel to an old stone building that may have in its day served as kitchen, or stables. That is where I sleep now, in a small room of my own. But upon the founding of our Order the old church was added on to and the two buildings connected, to form a cloister with arcades. The outbuildings, such as the stables and pilgrim's hut, added more recently, although already in disrepair. We are segregated by our habits, we in the choir in the old building and the lay sisters in white in the new. Lisette shares a cell with two other girls, but I have never learned their names.

As is the custom here, we are periodically moved, so that we do not think of our cells as our own. We are to switch tomorrow with the lay sisters, so it is likely Lisette should find herself in this room, or one like it, unaccompanied.

As for me, I can make some excuse to be alone in the stables. They know little of horses here, and if I insist that one is to be attended to, there is none to question me. I have made mention of the aged mare, and that she may be at her time. This elicits squeezed smiles of sympathy from the sisters. They cluck and nod. Of course.

Further, one of the sisters has died. She has not been here long, and she arrived hobbled. Blood poisoning, they say. Some women arrive like this, at the end of life, hoping that by committing to their year of novitiate and a life of service that they will be spared whatever fate might otherwise befall them. I imagine rarely that is the case. Regardless, she is laid out in the mausoleum, a short stone room beneath the chapel proper, accessible from the outside behind a stout oak door. I peeked in there once, my first week here, when curiosity had got the better of me.

Hilde, I think her name was. Not French, not even pretending. Just a woman, her feet in rags, walking with a stick. And now she is stitched in linen, shriven of her sins, and on a stone shelf beneath the ground, like an onion in a root cellar.

What I am about to do is monstrous.

———⟨●⟩———

I have no knife to cut poor Hilde out of her shroud-cloths, and they do not tear, so I unwrap her, gagging at the stench of death. Lisette does not watch.

There is no moon, and no light, but there is brass on the candlestick, and just enough shine to reflect what little starlight falls on whatever I need to see. I simply feel for the rest.

Hilde was a frail thing, but an uncooperative corpse. We three stagger clumsily from her tomb, the dance made more difficult as Lisette and I hold our veils over our faces. We stifle the temptation to offer prayers in our defense for what we are doing, what we are about to do, but I dare not think God would forgive us this particular trespass.

As my eyes adjust to the dark, I can see Hilde's slack jaw, her pale flesh like wax. This haunts me, as it should, that she should suffer such indignity.

Fortunately, I know the way by memory, or we should have had to grope our way down the corridor. But Lisette's cell has been my own, and in her bed we placed this death where my Lisette had breathed life into me once more. We arrange poor Hilde's hair as best we are able, and place a thin blanket over her. Lisette crosses herself, but I dare not. We tiptoe out of the room, and close the simple wooden door, retracing our steps outside.

We circle the monastery to the stables. The horses are shy and snort in the night, the stink of death on us, I suppose. Here there is a lantern still lit, as I had retired to the stables after Vespers.

We bundle straw and bind it tightly with rags, and then submerge the bulk of it in a bucket of water. Silently I open each stall and cluck the horses out with a gift of apple slices, and a pet on the nose. The stable doors open, we lead them each into the night, gently correcting those who wish to return to bed in confusion.

When the stable is empty, we take the sodden bundle and light the dry end with the lantern flame. Lisette walks it to the monastery door and places the now-smoking sheaf on the flagstones inside. Upon her return I gave her two now-saddled horses, made a match of straw, and set small fires around the barn. These catch quickly, too quickly for my timing, and we slap the other horses away as we mount.

It is a matter of heartbeats before the barn erupts into flame, the horses bolting, and the wet straw we lit inside the monastery pours black smoke beneath the main door. The night is ablaze, and, riding away, south along the pilgrims road to the stand of pines where I had buried our provisions, I am reminded of turning my back to the Palace-light, in my black cloak, to see the stars.

The fire thunders against the night air, like hoofbeats on our backs. Through the roar of the flames we make out the peal of bells. It will take some minutes before they discover the fire in the monastery itself is a false one, but the light from the stable fire, and the smoke, will confuse them long enough for our purposes. Fire is an animal thing.

The bass of the flames, the soprano of the bells, and the kettledrum of hooves on the old road. A music for the two of us, Lisette and I. South to the stand of pines.

——◄●►——

Saint-Etienne, south of Lyon.

We dare not go back to Marseilles. Saint-Étienne, or near enough to hear the bells. Lisette weeps. She cries for the vows she has broken, for our sins against God. She atones with each tear, each hungry morning, every bruise from every root.

At last this inn, and a chance to sleep the ache from our bodies. I try to bathe her but she shies from me, like a new horse. All the clucking and shushing I do, I can no more than brush her hair.

Rumour. I have not heard it, but my palace-girl instincts, honed from a life of gossip, can sense it. A rumour from the road.

Two nuns, they say. Grave-robbers. Arsonists. Horse-thieves.

Murderesses.

And for the first time in the history of rumour, entirely true.

We do travel as Salesian sisters, our escort delayed. No, not from Avignon, why? No, we have not heard of a fire. Black magic. Two girls bewitched. The whole monastery dead—no, alive, says another, save for one corpse placed in a bed. Dark magic and no doubt. And a trial at Aix.

Why Aix? The place curious. With all the curates and lawyers rattling around Avignon proper, a witch hunt beginning there seems obvious.

But no, Aix. Always Aix.

Will they know our names? Lisette used her own, and for my part I was Emilie. But of course, a matter of letters—how quickly a horse can run on such scandal—and I am La Maupin, the notorious whore of Marseilles who dresses like a man and fights like a man and takes women to my bed like a man. Yet a woman still. Such a terrifying, confusing creature I am to them.

Lisette cries in her sleep, like a kitten. I have a mind to gag her. I have kissed so many tears away, and yet they are endless. I sleep and she has saved them for me, her guilt, her tears. There is not even the thought of love from her.

She is a doll I have broken.

Once, when I was very young, a rider came in with three horses, re-wilded things with terror in their eyes. Their riders had been stalked and felled by wolves, the mounts left with great raking wounds down their flanks and their hearts clanking against their flesh like church bells. Horror in every pulse, and no blinder or feedbag or brushing could calm them. The horror had claimed them totally. Nostrils flaring not for safety, not for food, but always and forever catching the scent of wolf through their hammering pulse. Wolf, and that is the end of all things.

I pray (does it surprise you I pray?) Lisette will remember the woman she was, the woman for which we set the fire, and not just this little broken doll, alert for wolves.

She has left.

She had nothing, so it was simple enough to leave with everything she had while I slept. Alb and scapular, veil and cross, leggings and sandals. Not a single sous did she take with her, so a nun at last I suppose.

I declared war on God for her, and she wept and crept from our bed.

I picture her silent, rocking on the back of a hay rig, headed away from me.

The room is a disaster. Smokey candles the colour of fat. The road-goods still filthy, mud on the floor. My one good wig crushed to nothing, my gown stained unfit for a milkmaid. The breeches and tabard look at home here, at least, as do pistol and baldric and sword.

The sword makes everything simpler. It is night again, the bells tell me, though I can still see the town below in its little circle, hemmed in by a ring of green hills. The bell calls men to the tavern as much as it calls the pious to prayer. It calls the watch to their torches.

And it will call the swords to me.

Sore, but I have them, to a man. I must confess I am a little drunk.

I am ungentle. I rebuke a sentiment with a thrust, a tip with a cut, and those I disarm are rewarded with a blow to the nose with my pommel. The blood imparts the crowd a sense of communion, and there is much wine. Perhaps too much.

I am fine, for my part. A rolled shoulder. An extended knee which I shall feel in my buttock come morning. But I roared a challenge and they crowed like cocks and laughed, with the spinning of silver to the sawdust of the piste. The tavern-keeper declined to act as judge, but a portly and elderly fellow was found who had some experience, insisting dramatically that we all pray and drink to the King ahead of time. This was agreeable, particularly the drinking part.

One begins with a beat, and gets well within my point, although his lunge is hesitant. I slap his blade away with the flat of my other hand. My sword again on target, I let him play with it, working his way up to the hilt until he realizes that all the force is now with me, and a simple roll of my wrist has him nearly remove his own toes with the end of his blade. He jumps back and is more cautious after that. So much so that his fellows bid him withdraw, so they could get a turn.

Some come out of the gate with a flurry of wild cuts to the head, like little boys playing with sticks— stopped easiest with the ticking of a riposte, as though the sound itself was all they were seeking.

Wide open, of course, through all of this. Belly and chest. Heart and lung, throat and genitals, inner thigh. But their ferocious blows raining hard on the roof of battle, as they imagined it should be, and a single fist to the "button" of the chest, and they're in the sawdust, wheezing and baffled.

As the wine rolls in like a fog, both my technique and memory blur, the sword itself cuts through. All that remains is the familiar placement of muscle, the haze of their eyes, and two points in space—my blade, their blade. Nothing else matters. It is an escape the rosary could never match in its blissful obliteration of self.

The grave must be like this, I thought. Nowhere to go. No light, no music, just the minute awareness of this worm, here, scuttling across your rib cage to find some small incident of meat, heretofore unet. One thing, and one thing only. Like the moments in the blond, blond cave of Lisette's hair in the morning. Or the intake of breath before entering the stage. Beautiful.

Distracted, I find my blade buried in some farmboy's shoulder.

Shit.

He is still fighting, too hot or too drunk to realize what has happened. I rest the blade on my left shoulder and step forward, plucking his sword from his right hand with my own and dropping it, pinning his left hand to his side.

Don't move, I whisper.

It takes (it always takes) seconds for the crowd to become aware that the game has changed. I cannot tell if I have cut the artery under the clavicle or even nicked the upper part of the lung, which keeps it upright. Depending, he is either dead or alive, and merely has yet to be informed.

His compatriots clear and lower him to the table, the smallsword standing in his chest like a flag. The girl brings over a lantern and a pitcher—clearly, she is versed well-enough in such things.

Whiskey, I say, and linen.

When the whiskey arrives I shoot it back, and demand another.

This second I place on the table next to the clean-enough linen, torn I imagine from the girl's own chemise. Not filthy enough for a gown-end.

I dip my finger in the whiskey, and pull the sword straight out, plugging the hole again with my finger as I do so. He turns green from the pain, and his friends hold him down while I wiggle around a bit in the wound.

A little fishhook of bone, sheared off from the thrust. That would kill him if I failed to pull it out. Mercifully my fingernail catches it and flicks it out of him with a little spray of blood. I watch the blood well in the wound. Crimson and light, not too gummy, nor too watery. I felt the strings of muscle that connect the lungs to the rib, resisting the temptation to strum them like a harp.

I pack the linen tight into the wound, watch the red climb the little bone-white threads, the life itself escaping from him in filaments. I make the crowd silent, and place my head to his chest, as I have with horses a hundred times before. Even breaths without rasping, though he is sweating in a way I did not care for.

He will live. I pour the last of the whiskey over the bloodening rags in his chest and leave my winnings on the table.

Call a midwife, I say. Or a barber, or a seamstress. He'll live, save for any foolishness.

Here in the room, I barricade the door, should he turn cold and his friends hot.

I am a dangerous creature, and I can smell the fear on them. Perhaps Lisette could smell the danger on me, which first opened her to love, and then shut her like a book.

I must leave this place at dawn.

Between this valley and sea lie three great forests, Livradois, d'Auvergne, and Limousin, with only Limoges on the other side of this wilderness. Twenty days through the wood, or twelve days on the road to Poitiers.

And then what? This horse will be dead by then, unless I can purchase another along the way.

To Paris, eventually I assume, depending on whatever verdict the fine people of Aix have in store for me. So I set out for Poitiers, for now at least.

I hire two thugs, Pig and Boil. Pig was asleep downstairs when I found them, but I made the deal with a short, stout fellow with a boil on his neck. He roused his friend who snorted loudly on waking, hence, Pig.

It would be better to pay them in copper, so as not to whet any appetite in that regard, but silver sous are all I have. They simply have to keep me alive until Poitiers, and I am unconvinced they are altogether interested in the task. The role of a palace-daughter offers a protection, as does the role of two nuns a-road, though less so. A chaste pilgrimage. But even were I to pass as a boy, britches-clad and breasts-bound, one boy alone on the road is a succulent thing, ripe for plucking.

We are easy on the horses today and find, if not an inn, a stable and a room with some supper. Pig and Boil sleep with the horses, and it is the draw of a card if they are all there at dawn, whereupon I would find myself walking to Poitiers.

I shall have to make the best of my purchase, and drive hard tomorrow. Fifty miles if the horses can bear it, and leave the men too tired to try anything stupid if we have to sleep on the road. There is no steady palace-stream of merchants and their whispers, here. This is the road for those seeking to escape same. A fire is a beacon for such men.

Everything is brown. Straw and leather and dung and wood. Only when I sleep, when I dare sleep, is there any colour. The pink and blue of the costumes in the house ballets of my youth. The Greek heroines on every ceiling, all that naked baby-pink flesh staring down at me all my life, nudes comically in armour. Will they ever look upon me again? Athena in your helm atop your head, wearing only some tapestry and a spear, pointing at the dangling willies of cherubs. How absurd, in such a place as this, to think that other, magical places exist.

Every bone in my body has been hit by small hammers. I am a chorus of bruises and pangs, of sorrow and guilt, of heartbreak and chafing and exhaustion.

Ten nights of road ahead of me.

Four days. Rain. I dreamt of mussels and frites in Marseilles, and pink sugar for my coffee.

Pig and Boil and myself and the horses are still alive.

I smell like a goat.

Marechal has informed me that I have been sentenced to death.

I am to be burned. At the stake. Alive. Such is the judgment of the tribunal at Aix. Signed by no less a personage than de La Reynie himself, who must think he has me at last. It is not the part he would have me play, yet he has cast me nonetheless.

But Aix is a long way away. And there is none who would see me, here in half-empty Poitiers, that could raise a finger against me, and say there, there is La Maupin, arsonist and grave robber and murderess.

At least, I hope not.

I say Poitiers is half-empty, and that is no exaggeration. They built a new bridge here, but half the houses are shuttered, the shops barren. There are only two roads out of the city: one to Paris, the other to Quebec. The King has granted half the town lands in New France, and from here they have bundled up house and goods and children and left for the sea, into the West.

Perhaps I should go with them.

But I have just arrived, and enough days have passed that I have recovered so as to write, but not so many that memory fades. And I have not introduced Marechal to record. So.

The road. Pig and Boil, and the three of us staring into the trees, pretending to sleep, wondering if we should kill one another and be done with it. Each time they get up in the night to stoke the coals, or to piss on a tree, my eyes shoot open and I tighten my grip on my sword. Sleeping in fits, awaking in fear, and dreaming of Versailles, of Marseilles, of Avignon. Of Sérannes and Lisette and even, sometimes, of Louis.

I tell them that my husband is a merchant in Poitiers, that I had left him for reasons of my own, and that I was returning to him. Should they deliver me unharmed and intact (I stressed the word) that he would pay them each in livres, not the sous I had tossed them at the outset.

They did not wholly subscribe to this story at first. I suspect there is a hardness around my eyes that has crept there, and certainly in breeches I appear no merchant's wife. But I sing for them, hymns in Latin and opera in Italian, and for all the dirt under my nails in recent months, my voice is not one of poverty. They have wit enough between them to imagine I was worth something to somebody, and then only alive. Hence an uneasy truce, and near two weeks on the road. I keep them in wine when

I have the chance, or ale when I do not, and we lose none of the horses.

It is Marechal who saves me, at the end of the road, in Poitiers itself.

I dare not duel for money, not since Saint-Étienne. So I sing, and this is enough for stables and food for the three of us. The taverns improve in quality as we approach the city, with myself feeling increasingly unfit for company, and Pig and Boil harder to make excuses for.

But sing I shall, and Marechal—dear Marechal, the impresario with claimed connections to the most prestigious stages in Paris—who intervenes on my behalf. Who pays for my supper and sorts out Pig and Boil. At first, I think he has mistaken me for a grisette, but he is kindly and makes no intentions toward me in such a way. He reminds me a little of my husband in that regard. He is doughy, with a little cleft in his blob of a nose, and wears wigs fit for younger men.

First, he offers Pig and Boil employment, in some manner involving stepping away from a lady's ear. Likely murder, or some such. Anyway, whatever recompense they may have sought for not slaughtering me in the woods seems to have been satisfied by their new venture, and they are no longer my concern. Perhaps they have already drunk themselves to death.

Marechal takes me in, his intentions honourable but not entirely without benefit to him. He is familiar with Versailles and has fallen from some degree of grace, for reasons that remain his own (and presumably another's). But there is an audience, here, in the city, those whose lands and title and family names keep them here. And I shall be something new to them, he says.

So here in the larger of the rooms, which he has generously vacated on my behalf, he has summoned shoemakers and dressmakers and wigmakers, and I am restored to my role as palace-daughter and performer. Gone are my old things, save my sword and pistol (which I keep secret) and my velvet tabard and taffeta cloak, which were mud-spattered beyond recognition but are now returned to me pristine.

There is music to learn, after so long, and so different from singing the hours of convent life. Steps, and to dance again is a joy. The road at last has fallen from my feet.

Marechal has a young friend, a boy named Thevenard, who is vain and selfish but whose voice is lovely, and he has exquisite taste in everything. As a result he appears constantly disdainful, particularly where I am concerned. He is stick-thin and moves languidly. I should like him, if not for the incessant sneering. But like me he is a creature of Marechal's, and we do sing well together.

Marechal brought me to the obvious solution to my circumstance—my husband for money and Louis for my pardon. And so I write, with little to lose in either regard. I have written also to Marc for any news of Lisette—and of my affairs in Marseilles, and of poor Lilas. Mine since childhood, and mine at my hour of freedom from it, now lost to me it seems. I miss your velvet nose, my sweet Lilas!

I would not return to Marseilles even to do that which I have sworn, which is to kill Lisette's father and his men. While I would take such pleasure in that, it would not be worth the journey. Another vow I have broken; the first of my marriage, the second as a nun.

The musicians are here, and there is rehearsal.

I have won a battle with Marechal, with the aid of an unlikely ally in Thevenard. Marechal has been promoting our performance as some slice of palace entertainment, but I have rejected the gaudy colours and stiff forms for something lighter and prettier, with the softer colours I adore. I am to be something new to them, and so I shall be. Despite hours of dancing I have restored some of myself—the glass tells me I have made a wiry creature as a Visitandine sister and traveler. To have cakes again! I shall never go a day without marzipan, as it has gifted me once more with the softness of my body.

Not that there are any with whom to share it. I have no appetite where that is concerned. Every conceivable suitor has been shipped off to New France, or the war, or as a sort of hostage to Versailles. There are musicians, of course, and the footmen of the great houses where we travel to perform, but there are few of my station, man or woman, under the age of a hundred. Odd that my vows of chastity would take root only after I have left the monastery!

But of the houses. These are invariably beautiful, and there is an honesty in their antiquity one does not find in Paris. I find it charming, although before I would have preferred the fashion of making everything new. I may again. But these estates are worn and comfortable, like an old nightdress. Would that I could marry some ancient gentleman here and just grow fat where none could see me! But I suppose I would have done that with Jean-Baptiste, were I to. And I would miss performing, and I would no longer be La Maupin.

For all my passions, I have no desire to obliterate this thing I have become.

After a month, most everyone has seen our little pantomimes, and where they have been enthusiastically gobbled up, they too have demanded more. So, there is more music, new costumes, different scenes, and nights scheduled farther afield.

Between these I visit the cathedral here. Again, an ancient thing, more so I think than Notre Dame in Paris, although perhaps not. It has no organ, though, and screens of silk hint at a fire a handful of years ago. It is chilly, but I do so love the grandeur, the effort, of the stage and its performances, made holy with the addition of yet more silk and wine and gold.

Oh! And through the city were horsemen, and though they did not stop, I recognize them at once as musketeers. What is curious is that they wear neither the black of the King's guard nor the rarer grey of the Queen's, but a blue. The King has appointed a new fashion, it seems, and it would be no small blow to the men's purses to style themselves in new livery. But still, the blue is of the sky, and not of sapphire, so that seems entirely significant. Things are changing at Versailles, and I know nothing of them. Such an odd, odd thing. Perhaps I shall write to Elise and ask her of news. She of all people will not be scandalized to know me, although I imagine it is wisest to wait and not yet reveal my whereabouts? Odd, odd, as I say, and confusing, such times.

At the end of the month we are to journey some three days north of here, at Tours. Marechal has arranged a carriage for us, and friends along the way. How different from sleeping on tree-roots in the foreboding wood with Pig and Boil.

I do so hope Tours is a success. Marechal aspires, I think, to return to Paris.

Midnight. I am with a lone candle in an empty room, upstairs from an abandoned shop. It is freezing.

Men have come for me. The watch of Poitiers, with a warrant from de La Reynie, the Lieutenant General of Police. The cold, soulless creature is not waiting for me to return to Paris and tie myself to the stake.

Marechal, bless him, tells them that I had indeed been there (so many have seen me it would be impossible to lie) but that I had robbed him and fled. They are not entirely satisfied by this, and he fears they will return.

Unfazed, he tells me we will simply move up our appearance at Tours and leave in the morning. He seems almost happy about it. In a rare act of kindness, Thevenard himself has brought me soup and blankets, though he dared not use the fireplace.

Even the candle is too much flame for me tonight.

En route to Tours.

I have never mastered the art of riding in carriages. But Marechal seems almost joyful. He is not fleeing for his life.

We practice music. Thevenard finds the journey tedious.

I have to pee.

We are almost at Châtellerault, where we are to perform tonight.

I have a letter from Marc I will read when the coach stops lurching.

But I fear it is not good.

There is cake.

Châtellerault, where my sword was made. My father would come all the time, when I was little, and meet with the smiths here. They say it is the finest steel in all of France, and with a King's commission my father would order blades by the hundred.

They are very kind to me, here. The town itself is pretty and fashionable, and well maintained: this is because the King himself owns much of it. I was practically nursed on such politics, and the whole affair is transparent to me.

What I mean is this. The wigs here are towering, and new. There is fresh gold applied to the statuary. New fountains in new marble, and all the hammering and sawing of my youth.

To pay for it all, of course, the battlements and bridges are sold to the King. The nobles have all been moved into the Palace, where the King can keep an eye on them—only castoff wives and younger brothers are kept in the family estates. Long before I was born, the nobility rose up against him when he was barely more than a boy. But a peace was made, and now he has them right where he wants them, does the Dancing King. He has enslaved them through beauty.

As a result, the chateau in which we stay and perform is aching in its efforts to look like the Palace, with the same charming failures as Poitiers, although less rustic with each mile that leads closer to Versailles. Still, I can lie back on the bed's satin, see the painted figures gallivanting on the ceiling, and imagine myself home. There is even a helmeted heroine, some confusion of Athena, whom I always pretended to be as a girl.

So an hour's peace between introductions and avuncular flirtations, and rehearsal. The musicians arrive with a clatter shortly after we do ourselves. I bundle sword and pistol under the bed, and re-read the letter from Marc.

Lisette returned to her father, duly chastened and chaste and chastised. She was married off pretty much immediately, the bishop having no doubt been persuaded to release her from her vows with the aid of gold. Marc says nothing of the man she has wed, but I can well imagine. Fat, dull, strict, old, rich, and no doubt too stupid to see the treasure she is. She will never kiss him as she kissed me. Hers is now a kind of death—more so than when she was in the monastery. Yet she lives.

As for all the beauty of the salon, which we so painstakingly imagined and brought to life, it has been sold off, even the wallpaper, to pay for my debts. Marc himself found a home for Lilas, traded to one of my former students at the salle. This saddens me, but I know it could be far worse. Marc's father could have bought him to punish me. That is perhaps what I would have done, so I am grateful at least for this oversight. Not a lack of spite, just a lack of imagination.

There has been no word from my husband or my Count—but how could there be? Any letters would be sent to Poitiers. However, we have livres enough for now, thanks to my voice, and I am at least a town ahead of de La Reynie's police.

Lisette and Lilas and Sérannes, all lost to me. But there can be no sadness now, lest it creep into my voice. I have sent for lemon tea and pink sugar.

———◖●◗———

Marechal says we must leave for Villeperdue before any of our generous Harcourt hosts can brag about being presented the notorious (!) La Maupin. I was gifted with a darling porcelain box, for powder, that threatens to crush like an eggshell. Indeed, it is the colour of a robin's egg, with a picture of a lady on a swing, worked in white.

I forget, in the face of generosity and elegance, that men on the road behind me are coming to arrest and kill me. What a curious thing, to lapse in memory.

No noble estate awaits us, midway between here and Tours. Just a tavern, owned by a friend of Marechal's, he says. No performance tonight, and it is ever so slightly off the main road that there will be less fear of de La Reynie.

Back to the carriage, to suffer the tedious sighs of Thevenard. Although he sang beautifully last night.

<hr />

Villeperdue proves to be nothing more than a bucket to piss in.

The road is nearly impassible, rutted early for the season, and after the rattling of the carriage we are all lucky to have teeth in our heads. At least de La Reynie's men would not think to look for us here.

Thevenard keeps a deck of cards in a silk box of the palest yellow, which serves as a card table between our laps in the carriage. Thevenard always wins. It is tedious. I used to quite enjoy card games.

At least there is a bottle of Champagne–a gift from the Harcourts–which is not fashionable because the English drink it, but I adore the bubbles, and the sweetness. Champagne every day, I say. And marzipan. Then I can stomach even the autumn road.

There is nothing here. Some farms, and one tavern that stinks of the road and pig shit. A proper hotel down the road, but Marechal has some business here with his friend. There are sea creatures that come ashore at night, like crabs. Marechal is such a creature, living as he has between two worlds. I have become such a thing myself, I suppose. Some part of me wishes I had trouble sleeping in such a place as this. I wish it was less familiar, less comfortable. Yes, give me pink sugar whenever possible, but a tavern-room or convent walls are better than bracken for a bed, which I have known for too many nights.

Thevenard is sulking in his room.

I am going downstairs to get a drink.

They are louts, I think, and when one of them bumps into me coming back from behind the tavern (I stepped out to relieve myself and I suspect he'd done the same thing), I take perhaps too much offense. We quarrel, and this alerts his friends who come to investigate the shouting.

I would say he drew his sword first, but my temper is up. I get this way, so I cannot say for certain. At least once the blade is in my hand my head clears somewhat, and I see that he is no lout, but a gentleman. An officer. Cavalry, by the stance he takes and his preference for the high guard.

And two of his friends, who are at first alarmed and then amused. A girl with a sword. And I want to slice the smirk off their stupid faces. I press a feint against my opponent and deliver an imbroccata to his friend's arm, which makes him draw, and his friend, too.

Now there is me and my temper and the wine, the three of us, against the three of them.

A few cuts and nothing serious against the first two, whom I have successfully disarmed despite their obvious skill—but I overstep for the third and instead of just nicking him in hopes of a disarm, I staple him where the shoulder meets the clavicle. Either right through or just missing the artery there. But there is a glint of steel and blood coming out of entirely the wrong side of him.

And then I am tackled into the mud, my head knocking hard against the stones of the tavern wall, reeking of piss.

It is Marechal who throws me, and then hauls me up under my arms and drags me from the scene. I am in a rage, screaming and clawing at him, but there is rather a lot to Marechal, and he is behind me. Due to some wrestler's hold all I can do is flail away like a mad thing.

Then temper falls away, and shame descends on me like an oily curtain.

And he puts me to bed and bolts the door. He is asleep still in a chair he's dragged in front of it, so there is no escape for me.

My head is pounding, and I am dying of shame. But I shall die corporally should they ride and to the main road, and word gets out of a mad swordswoman stabbing random cavalry officers.

Marechal is furious. I wish I were dead.

No, I do not. If death was for me, I would have stood there and not defended myself. But wine clouded my head, and now there is again blood and insult and angry families.

I need more water, and more sleep.

He is alive. d'Albert is the name of the man I wounded yesterday. The other two have names, which I was told, but I did not hold onto them.

Marechal has been silent. I want him to scream and call me a foolish, idiot girl and drunkard, no better than Pig and Boil with whom he first found me. But he looks at me with his giant kind eyes, and I have broken something inside him. Some trust.

I take too much wine, I say.

You do, he says.

No more, I tell him.

And he nods gravely.

That is the entirety of our exchange.

I remember the chaste, pale girl I would play at Mass. I spend the morning picking away at the frill of my blue silk gown, to give it a plainer neck. I tame my hair with the help of a girl fetched from a farm, after showing her how, pulling my hair back to look like there was more of it that I was hiding beneath a modest bun and a white linen cap. My smallest pearls. In the dirty glass here, I look enough like the contrite girl and less like the madwoman of the night before.

I have called for a carriage, although a single horse would be faster. But I am determined to go to the hotel and apologize, to beg his forgiveness and work whatever miracle I may in that regard.

For a miracle is what I need. If word of this gets to de La Reynie, not too far behind me I am certain, then I am a dead woman.

This performance must be perfect. My life depends on it.

In this, I have failed.

First, this is all Marechal's fault that we are here at all and not in Tours. Secondly, that we stayed in that wretched road-tavern as opposed to the very acceptable hotel scarcely three miles east is something of an outrage. None of this would have happened without whatever dark dealings kept him skulking around such a pisspot.

I arrive and feign nervousness–which I must admit was not entirely counterfeit, but I play it up a bit. I present myself to the Maître and bow deeply until he remembers to take my hand. Court manners, as out of place as an orchid in a pigpen.

Then I ask to see Monsieur d'Albert, that I bear a message for him which must be delivered in person. As a finishing touch I ask him to escort me to the room, and if he would be so kind as to remain outside the door so as to vouchsafe certain things which need no mention, propriety and blah de blah. I have him on the hook.

It is misfortune that at that moment, descending the stairs, is one of the lieutenants with whom I had crossed swords. He fails to recognize me at first, but

I am pretty enough that he looks at me a heartbeat too long. And then recognition.

He is in that dullard's rage men enter when they have been embarrassed. A dangerous and ox-like mood, clumsy and callous. He roars and slanders me, leaving the Maître quite taken aback, but drives me out of the place and belabours me even as I shut the door of the carriage.

I am at a loss. I must get to d'Albert.

I have not failed. *She* has failed. The girl I pretended to be.

I have a plan.

Oh, I know I have asserted this before, and it has not always gone in my favour, but this is a good plan.

Thevenard is useless, as he dresses more like a girl than I do. But between my breeches and a borrowed shirt and cap from the tavern-girl's brother, I will serve as a messenger boy.

I have even applied some soot under my eyes and across my chin. One good stroll through mud and pig shit and I shall pass adequately for belonging to this place. Villeperdue indeed. A last look at the glass. Failing this, I will take some peasant girl as my bride and surprise her on our wedding night. Now *there* is a scandal for a small town.

But no.

The boy I am will pass where the girl was barred.

And so I am in love.

Marechal and Thevenard leave for Paris. There is an address, a Café Procope, where I can find them later, should I need to. But Thevenard is bound for the opera of the Academie Royale de Musique and Marechal (and his purse) is determined to take him there.

My ruse works as intended. I pass unnoticed through the hotel with only a brief and apathetic interrogation by the Maître, who neither recognizes me nor looks at me long enough to try. A boy, with a message for a soldier recovering from his wounds. The Maître probably thinks the boy in front of him cannot read the paper in his hand, if he thinks of him at all.

But once in d'Albert's room, my cap off and a rush of apology. It comes out of me in a torrent, and I think I am babbling. All craft robbed of me.

Shirtless, he is beautiful. I can tell by his skin there was no infection—he would be pale and sweating, but he looks, I do not know, perfect. Save for a wrapped shoulder which was clean and expertly done, pinning his left wrist to his right hip, wound 'round. Someone sensible has seen to him. Someone military.

He laughs. I did not know what to expect, but the appearance of his assailant dressed as a boy—a decidedly filthy boy at that—causes him to laugh so hard he winces. And at this I rush to him to aid him back to sitting on the bed, and pour him wine.

He asks me to share and I decline, pointing at my head. Tenderly his fingers brush in my hair looking for the bruise Marechal left, or rather, the tavern wall had left after Marechal extracted me from my own folly.

And then I do something I had not done for a very long time. I talk.

d'Albert is a swordsman, a horseman. We speak of blades and horses, of Versailles (his blood is of the Duke of Luynes and so he, too, spent many days visiting his father, held captive as they all are, pinned like a butterfly to a card in the King's collection).

He is a Louis, but of course I shall never call him that. My Count d'Armagnac shall be the only Louis. And so for me, he is d'Albert.

Blond, and blue-eyed, pale as a cornflower. His hands are broad and strong, and he listens as I tell him everything—except Sérannes—but of Lisette and poor Lilas, and the convent and de La Reynie and how in all the world a palace-girl with a gift for steel and song should arrive in the muddy bootprint that is Villeperdue.

And as he listens he brushes my too-short hair from my face and wipes the tears from my cheeks. He sends for food to the room and we speak, for hours and hours, of his time in Saxony and his home in the valley, just west of Tours. Scarcely a day from here.

Later when he kisses my neck and my collarbone, he kisses above my breast and the small scar there, and laughs that I had given him a matching one. He calls me Emilie, a nun's name, but a lover's name, he says. A secret name. I love how his lips part when he says it, the tongue lightly on the teeth after.

I have never known a friend such as d'Albert, and that we are lovers seems almost incidental. I swear we shall never tire of each other's company.

I have sent for my things from that awful tavern. I still blush in shame when I think of the place, and that I would near ruin this beautiful man, in whose arms I sleep.

I do not know what is to become of us, but this room is all the world to me.

He is anxious to ride, despite the ache in his shoulder. I change the dressing of the wound and it is healing clean enough, both entry and exit. Well-stitched, testament to a skilled barber, and d'Albert complains that both are itching to the point of madness, and that is the best sign.

Today we ride, briefly, out to the farms west of the inn. Away from the mud and scraggly, menacing trees, there are rolling hills, and little villages in bowls of valley, rustic and picturesque. I tell him we should buy a farm here and raise chickens, and he jokes that he is afraid of chickens. So, I bawk at him loudly as I chase him on horseback, and we laugh through the fields.

He sleeps after love.

d'Albert's lieutenants (with whom I crossed swords) have been made to forgive me by their captain, and they have both been utterly courteous with me, entirely gracious with their pardon, and completely pre-occupied with the local girls. They are generous with wine, though this I have forsaken until I can entirely forgive myself for my recent fiasco.

Letters have begun to arrive for him, and he has been discussing matters with the two of them. Brows furrowed. But when d'Albert turns back to me he is lighter, and an endless font of affection and humour.

I have, during these hours of planning and military dispatches, rather set myself up as mistress of the place. I have shared with the cook some of the more current dishes, rearranged one of the salons of the hotel, and have spoken at length with the Maître about a more fashionable livery for the staff. They are all delighted with the changes I have suggested. As the season is turning, I thought of hosting a soiree here, perhaps a performance? But who would come? And I am supposed to be in hiding from the police, of course.

I do so love these languid days, of sleeping in, reading and loving. We ride in the afternoons, after d'Albert has met with his men. Four more have arrived, and they are looking at maps. It gives me more time to write, or to take a horse out alone (I leave my sword in our room, but I am careful to conceal my pistol), but it does take away my precious hours with d'Albert.

He has been summoned away.

I have begged him to leave with me, to run away to New France, across the ocean. He laughs at this, kisses my forehead, like I am a child.

Tomorrow we leave together for Paris, and he is to rejoin his regiment there and prepare for some expedition in Bavaria. Having already placed too many holes in my lover myself, I shall be quite upset if some foreign cannon should damage him further. How to tell such a man to be careful? We are not careful things, by nature.

For the first time that I have been in love, I do not fear the loss of it. This love is different, as though d'Albert and I have already spent a lifetime together, and while we are both of us creatures of passion, there is a fondness, a solidity to our love which is less incendiary. Like we are ancients, looking with sweetness upon the ruins, and raising a glass to our memories of one another. Poignant. How strange it all is.

I will take a horse, and my belongings will follow behind by carriage, which will arrive at Jean-Baptiste's apartments. A week's ride. Five days at speed.

I do not know if I dare enter the city. When d'Albert and I are alone it is easy to forget that there are those who wish me burned alive, like Joan of Arc.

What this world does to women who dare raise a sword.

I did not know where else to go, so I enter Paris, in Marais. Louis' house is here, and I take refuge.

The ride is not onerous, even pleasant. To ride with good horsemen, who care for their mounts and tack! After the first day, none ask if I could keep up. The pace is brisk but not overwhelming, either for myself or any of the horses.

They are kind, too, and quick, the men. d'Albert sends a rider ahead to find a camp, and he returns with a spot in mind. We arrive, and within minutes there is water fetched for, tents erected, a fire lit, vines cut back, and two men circling in a wide arc to look for other travelers or road-men. All of it as it should be, with deliberation and care like the competent men backstage in a quality theatre. If singing fails me, I shall join the cavalry.

Upon arriving in the city, I decide to enter at d'Albert's side. The captain's woman. Miraculously my taffeta cloak is brushed to gleaming, and no evidence of five days of road upon us.

But there is a good-bye as he calls me Emilie one last time, with his horse returned to d'Albert's men. A kiss, and such a kiss! I should go to Mass and light a candle for that kiss, that it might return to my mouth. My captain alight. My friend.

How strange to part without heartache. Not like Sérannes' hot-blooded departure, nor Lisette's cold one.

But here I arrange myself, in the streets of Paris, with a small bundle (d'Albert's crimson jacket, so that I could have his arms around me despite our distance), pistol and sword, and nowhere to go. Except home, of course. All my things will be there in a few days. But servants talk, and even if they do not, grocers do. More coal for the fire all of a sudden and people wonder who comes and who goes. No, not to Jean-Baptiste, even if there is a ghost of him there.

Thus I inquire at a wine shop which I know stocks many of the better cellars, which house is that of the Count of Armagnac? And I accept the gift of a fine Burgundy, and of an escort, to find myself at the doorstep of my Louis' home in Marais.

My part here is a familiar one, the costume of cloak already around my shoulders. I present myself, discreetly, as the Count's mistress, without a word of dishonesty. And I send a note that I await his arrival here.

In the meantime I set to making the most of myself, bathing and polishing, the servants attending to my wig and shoes. A girl was sent for, but a proper maid arrived, and dressed me, powdered and painted.

As a finishing touch: a simple yet unsubtle silk ribbon about my throat, in the most referential shade of pale pink.

While I do not receive a note in reply, the house is suddenly abuzz. Servants fetching and cleaning, stoking fires and lighting candles. I know the sound of staff with an imminent arrival.

We dine. That is all.

Oh, we speak at length. Louis lets it be known with some subtlety that he is aware of my connection to Sérannes and the duel at the Carmelites, though he does not mention this directly. He seems amused by the whole affair.

He has been expecting me. Not just today, from my letter, but from those I had sent from Poitiers. Regardless, he has in his possession a copy of a letter presented to the King, for my pardon.

Impossible, he says, that I should burn for this impossible crime. Besides, the warrant for my arrest is for a "Monsieur d'Aubigny," for clearly in the eyes of the tribunal no woman could have attempted such a thing. Not merely impossible, but inconceivable. It has all made for the best Palace gossip.

Did I really, he asks, seduce a nun, rob a grave, steal horses, and burn down a convent? He makes it sound so simple, all together like that. So while I have been "excused" from this affair, no pardon is to be granted for this "Monsieur La Maupin of Marseilles"—this notorious gentleman who does not and never did exist.

Louis returns to the Palace, and I am free to stay here until I can make amends with my husband, which the good Count insists I do.

I will sleep, as I am beyond exhausted. From travel, from relief, from saying good-bye to d'Albert.

I shall pray tonight that I dream of the monastery. A simpler life without so many men.

I know I ought to remain here. It is pleasant enough, the staff hospitable. They are from the palace, most of them, and understand the place of a mistress. There is no scorn from them, no false propriety, as they assume that my task is to put their master in a more favourable mood, generally. And so there is kindness, and Champagne (which I decline) and marzipan. Little dogs everywhere, and so little black turds behind all the furniture, which keep the footmen bowing up and down in a constant effort to define parlour from stable.

I ought to remain here.

I ought, too, to find this Café Procope, and see if there is word from Marechal (and by extension Jean-Baptiste or Marc, as anything for me was to be forwarded to him). I could send a maid, I imagine, or a footman to fetch word. I do not know where this place is, and if a maid would venture, or return.

All right. Venture I shall. I call for a carriage, and as a precaution conceal both smallsword and pistol under black taffeta once again, the weight of it all reminding me that I am a dangerous woman.

──────◆──────

Rue des Fossés-Saint-Germain-des-Prés: the street is not particularly threatening, but seedy enough to be interesting. I could have sent a maid, after all, but glad I did not.

This so reminds me of the little café in Marseilles, save the aroma of mussels. Caved ceiling like a wine cellar, though chandelier-and-mirror bright, the light from the street spilling back. Perfectly square marble tables, cool to the touch. But the coffee is good, and there is pink sugar, and sorbet. There is a stack of letters behind the bar with a note: La Maupin. Marechal's handwriting. I shall go through them later, I think. It is enough now for there to be somewhere to go, and to not be there. What freedom in this.

Marechal and Thevenard are at the Chateau de Saint-Germain-en-Laye, an hour west of the city. This is where all the new performances debut–before settling here, the operas were all being set in tennis-courts—and Fanin (the protegé of the sparkling Lully) is staging another *Cadmus & Hermione*.

Hermione! Daughter of the gods. I know this so well and have performed parts of it in the house-plays ever since I was a little girl. I must get an audition–Marechal knows everyone, the matter should be simple.

There is something here from Louis, although I think written before we spoke, and there too is something from my husband.

I shall read it in the carriage. But I require more cake and coffee. I feel almost foolish for being so armed. Paris is the safest place in the world for me now. I shall remake it with my voice, as I once made it with my sword.

There are crumbs down my dress, and I think I shall move to the small tables outside, so that the little birds there may dine on these, my smallest accidents.

Jean-Baptiste's letter says nothing except to inquire after my health and happiness. This is of course saying everything. He is an unwavering banner of forgiveness of all my sins. I have been to confession and Mass and been there shriven, but it is one thing to be at peace with God, and quite another to be at peace with one's husband.

I will not wait until morning before going to the theatre. I dined here in Marais and changed very little, except to remove my wig and do my hair, now brushing my shoulders. It is, I think, boyish and arresting, a fashion of my own. I will be damned if I am to go unnoticed and take some chorus role.

The carriage is here.

How foolish I am to forget such an obvious thing.

Chateau de Saint-Germain-en-Laye is of course the estate which my husband, Jean-Baptiste, manages for the King, who was born here. It is also the home of the theatre, the Master Lully's personal laboratory in which he concocts the future of all art and spectacle for France, and thereby the whole of Europe.

I arrive and inquire as to the M. Fanin but am informed he is busy. I ask if M. La Maupin was present, and he has been sent north on some business of the King's. I ask after Marechal, and am met with unfamiliarity, if not tediousness. Finally, I ask after Thevenard, and am told he is in rehearsal, though no escort is provided for me. Once

I am appraised as a player, a hand-wave is all I am afforded.

The Chateau is definitely a creature of its time, shackled to a previous age, yet, as the Palace, under constant construction in pursuit of fashionability. The gardens are impressive for this part of the city and seek to mirror those of Versailles—although obviously on a more modest scale.

The younger girls, first, in heavy powder. A gaggle of them. This is how I find the theatre, or at least a door to it. After that, rough workmen, hauling in barrels and sandbags and buckets of paint; dyed feathers in the gravel, crushed underfoot; the strains of music.

I know the overture as well as I know my own name. I sail into the sea of players like a ship into a harbour, my neck long and my steps deliberate. All part for me as I look for Thevenard.

I find him easily enough, and he seems bored to see me. There is little sense in making conversation—we are not friends, and he wants nothing from me. I do ask him about Marechal, and this is met with a shrug. Thevenard is where he intended to be, here, at the Academie, and that is all that matters to him. I ask for an introduction to M. Fanin, and he reluctantly agrees.

We walk past the chorus, mostly younger players still sorting out positions and costumes, flirting with one another outrageously. Lewd fawns gyrating their goat-legs against the tambourine girls, who swat them away with a laugh.

Fanin appraises me briefly and assumes, accurately, that I wished to audition. He reaches out and touches my chin, turning it to the light, and asks of my voice. He seems disappointed when I tell him I am a contralto. But I press, saying that I know every note of Hermione.

Look amongst you, he says, waving. As do they all.

I say I should like to sing for him, and he makes me time for tomorrow. I thank him and bow, and as I leave he asks me my name.

La Maupin, I tell him.

Madame? Mademoiselle?

La Maupin, I say.

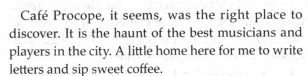

Café Procope, it seems, was the right place to discover. It is the haunt of the best musicians and players in the city. A little home here for me to write letters and sip sweet coffee.

I have been cast—not as Hermione, as I had hoped (though fair, it being a soprano role)—but as Pallas Athene. Athena, who looked down at me, her Spartan helmet perched atop her head, all through my childhood. Goddess of Wisdom. Well, what little wisdom I possess is hard-earned.

I have friends here. Marthe, who is so beautiful it makes it a challenge not to kiss her more than I may, and Fanchon, who is also blond and lovely. They sing magnificently, although when Fanchon moves off the stage she is rather clunky and graceless. Only when painted and lit does she come alive. Sometimes when they laugh or brush the hair from their collarbones there is a pang in my chest that reminds me of Lisette. I could fall too easily in love with Marthe Le Rochois. Our Hermione, of course.

Thevenard arrives here at the café but stays only briefly. He has a sort of camp-follower, one Dumenil, a dullard who smells vaguely of boiled vegetables. Dumenil somehow has attached himself to this production, and so I must suffer his tedious presence daily. He is entirely artless, and he makes grotesque passes at Fanchon Moreau, with whom he is inexpertly in love. And he rudely takes snuff at the table, only to sneeze and spatter snot over everything.

However, a glance at Marthe is all that is required to return the light to any room. She smells like summer when I embrace her. But always sisterly, with a bat of a fan and a compliment to dress or bauble. Have I learned some caution? Perhaps it is Athena who watches over me now.

I have encamped to Jean-Baptiste's apartments in advance of the return of the Comtesse d'Armagnac to Marais. It is just as well. Louis did not return to take advantage of my residency there, so it was best if I retreated to more secure quarters. Having reconciled with my husband, I am but a short distance away.

Much of what I wished for had arrived in my absence. New wallpaper and draperies, new china. The right candles, which alone makes all the difference in the world. The new chaises are still wrapped and stacked in the corners, with the heavy medieval oak monstrosities squatting in the center of the room, but these should be removed to the attic by the time I come home.

No rabbits, though. Perhaps it was a silly idea, and would only make my heart ache for my quiet days in Marseilles. Or perhaps I should wait until Spring. No matter.

My days have suddenly become fittings and rehearsals, introductions and memorization. New forms on such a piece as this, a favourite of the King and one of Lully's finest *tragedies*. Cadmus, King of Thebes, and Hermione, daughter of the gods, who sits across from me now in the form of the delicious, swan-throated Marthe.

When not in rehearsal, we are a tribe of glittering savages in Procope, spilling sugar and gossip and rubbing our sore feet. We all have grand homes to which we may return. And we choose not to.

Were Jean-Baptiste at the Chateau I would impose, and take rooms there. As it is, there is some small journey, daily, west to Saint-Germaine-en-Laye, and while sometimes I am accompanied by my friends, more often I am not. I ought simply take a horse, and propriety be damned. I'd be there in half the time.

Tomorrow, then.

Rehearsal today is arduous. There is some rope-work, as I am to descend from the clouds, while singing. To hold the core of one's body erect while being yanked on by hemp and rough stagehands, and look elegant and composed and sing without so much as an "oof" or swearing at this or that thick-fingered buffoon is no slight endeavor. The trick (and one they have yet to master) is to have both sides of the performer's hips descend at the same rate. This is a two-rope, two-handed procedure. But if these idiots are not drunk, I swear they have been kicked in the heads by horses, and recently. They have me bobbing above the stage like a fish on a hook.

There is, however, a moment I enjoy, even being in harness, suspended above the stage. We have a moving sun now that traverses the scene, and lovely billowed clouds of shimmering taffeta. As I hang in mid-air, my Spartan helm perched atop my head, I am Pallas Athena herself. I can see all the world beneath me, gods and men, musicians and seats for the audience, the maestro and chorus and players and workmen. All. And I above them. Perceiving. Understanding at this curious remove. A goddess.

They will adore me.

But ah! my ribs ache!

Dumenil.

He is in his cups, after rehearsal, and makes another vulgar display of his affections for Fanchon, of whom I am suddenly protective, and I think he frightens her. He tears at her dress and attempts to kiss her, and she rebuffs his advances.

I grab his wrist and bend it forward—this is no exotic trick, it is how you remove a dagger from the hand of a pinned opponent, entirely elementary— and it puts fire in his eyes. I think he makes to strike me, but thinks better of it when I neither flinch nor withdraw. I increase pressure until the ghost of regret flickers behind his face. He leaves, sulking.

I should leave the matter there. But such is not my nature.

I wait a few minutes, mostly to compose myself. I make polite excuses, and follow Dumenil into the street.

He carries no sword, but he is never without a baton. Perhaps he fancies himself some maestro, and constantly bashes the floor with the thing or waves it about while aggrandizing himself, the tedious wretch. Regardless, I am unarmed, and as I approach, he dares point his stick at me with menace, if little resolve.

This does not end here, I say.

He of course sputters a torrent of words I have heard before; I suspect every woman who has ever challenged such a half-man has heard before. Slut. Whore. Bitch. There is never much imagination invested in these transactions.

I simply approach him, and as he darts his stick to my face, I pluck and twist it from his grasp. He puffs up, daring me to strike him. So I reply. First to the button in the center of the chest, to take the wind out of him. Then a crack to the collarbone, to remove the arm as a threat. Lastly a strike to the nose, to break it, which slows breathing as the blood flows, and restricts vision as the eyes bruise to shutting. He more or less slides to his knees.

At this point, a blow to the head would kill him. I consider against it.

Give me your watch, I say.

He looks at me blankly through dimming eyes, and snorts in confusion.

Your pocket watch, I say. With the one arm he could still move, he dangles his watch toward me on a chain and I snatch it. Then I remember.

Your snuffbox, I instruct. Give it to me.

He complies, wincing and cringing, fumbling for it, and hands it over. A small silver thing I had come to associate with ill manners generally.

I cross the street without looking back, and find a waiting carriage. I drop the stick, slightly bloodied, into the gutter.

As soon as the coachman shuts the door, the rush of the affair shoots through the back of my hands, my heart racing, and all I can do is laugh at the absurdity, clutching my prizes of watch and snuffbox, like a gutter-thief. I bathe when I get home and forget about it all by bed-time.

—◄●►—

This morning I take a horse to the theatre, so much quicker, and arrive warmed for dancing, and I care not a whit that such transportation is considered eccentric. Odd how a woman on horseback gathers no notice north to south, on any of the roads through the city (so long as she is accompanied), but riding west to St. Germaine is viewed as shocking. It is a route for carriages. But convention bores me so.

Anyway this morning upon my arrival there is a great to-do in the dressing room, and a small crowd clusters around the tedious Dumenil, seated at his vanity applying make-up to his bruises.

Four of them, he says.

And the younger girls lean forward to gingerly touch the bruising and bump on his broken, squashy nose.

Great brutes of men, he says. Monstrous, misshapen heads, with teeth as big as your thumb, he says.

I gave the first a proper rebuke, he says. He'll not be a-horse for some weeks, he says, and they laugh.

The second left me some of his teeth as a thank-you, he says.

And the girls' hands all shoot to their mouths. Dumenil has his audience.

But the other two stepped over their fallen comrades, and so rushed me to the ground, to belabour me as you see from my wounds, he says.

And oh they cluck over him like hens, touching the filthy and poorly-wrapped bandage on his shoulder like some holy relic. Like he was some dashing cavalier from the front in Germany. Like he was d'Albert, with a war story and a medal.

Thanks be to a merciful God, he says, their intentions were not murderous but larcenous. For they seized upon my watch and snuffbox, and thought only of their safety should I regain my feet!

And at this he looks at them expecting applause, and near receives it. It is all I can stand.

I cut through them. Stride into a crowd as though it is not there, and it will not be. Approaching his vanity I drop off both pocket watch and snuffbox, as though they were pennies for a barmaid.

I look into his swollen eyes, and give him my most innocent smile, the demure smile of the girl I played in Mass each morning. Immaculate. Blameless, and

not a thought in my pretty head. And then I give
him a curtsy the depth of a mouse-hair, turn on the
ball of one foot, soundlessly, and leave.

I can hear their gaze on the objects on the table,
the evidence of his lie. It is perhaps the wickedest
thing I have ever done, judging only from the sheer
satisfaction of the act.

Delicious.

Shaking. Nerves. Why should I be nervous?

It is my debut here at the theatre in perhaps
twenty minutes. Marthe looks absolutely dazzling
as Hermione, and all surely will fall in love with her
as I have.

My head is more pins than hair, trying to keep
this helmet in place. It is ridiculously heavy, and my
only concern is that it will fall to the stage while I
descend from the ropes. And I pray the stagehands
have not been drinking, or at least that they don't
begin until the curtain rises, which should give it
some time to hit the blood.

If they drop me, I shall slaughter them cheerfully.

Elise wrote to me she is in the audience. After,
she will meet me at Café Procope, where we are to
have some little party. I told her of my fondness for
Champagne, and she teased me it was wine fit only
for an English alehouse.

I'll slap her after the show!

Why am I so nervous? I think I shall be sick.

That is the call.

Flawless. I so wish to bottle this moment. To be part of something so perfect, so beautiful.

I am majestic.

They adore me.

La Maupin. The applause is ringing in my ears. La Maupin, they cry.

La Maupin!

And after such lightness, my heart is heavy.

After another performance, which was again flawless, or, at least, if anything was less than perfect it was not while I was onstage, we retire again to Café Procope. And there is news.

Lully is dead. The voice of France and all music has died.

The songs we thrust out into the audience, past the rows and rows of mirrored candles, these are all Lully. The violins in the halls of my youth are Lully. The first steps I took as a dancer, my first costume, my first role, even as an infant, all Lully. And Lully is dead.

Tomorrow is my eighteenth birthday, and Lully is dead.

It is not too much treason, I think, to suggest that the King himself is a song Lully wrote once. Oh, we all know he fell out of favour, even years before my birth. But still, in all the little details from the height of music stands to the tuning of instruments, these are all to the blueprints, still, drawn out by Lully. The genius who invented my life—all our lives, we of the theatre. We of the Café Procope on the

Rue des Fossés-Saint-Germain-des-Prés, we are the creatures of Lully.

We do not know if the theatre is to fall silent in mourning, or if we perform tomorrow—music in defiance of mortality. Beauty in the face of sorrow. Or to surrender to sorrow. We do not know.

And in the midst of tears and coffee and cakes and sugar, and more tears (players are not known for their emotional restraint) there is yet more grim news.

d'Albert has been arrested. He wrote to me here at the Café.

Returning from the front, he was duelling. I do not know if this was between friends, or in anger, or over some trifling of regimental pride, but still, the King has forbidden this and so my d'Albert is now imprisoned. What is the penalty for duelling? Considering this is a law I myself have broken countless times, I ought to know. So, another thing I do not know:

Whether there is to be music after Lully's death, or what is to come of d'Albert.

The other night seeing Elise again was a joy, and there was gossip and there was Champagne and Marthe came and kissed me, she was so happy, so radiant, and Elise and I talked until she found distraction in the form of some fop to toy with, and off she went. And that was no simple joy, that night, but a nourishment of the soul. Old friends and new, the triumph of the stage and the kiss of a pretty girl, and "all the world reveres the God who makes our pleasant days" as we sing in *Cadmus & Hermione*, by the brilliant Lully, who is now dead.

I shall write to my poor d'Albert.

Packed, as they say. *Cadmus & Hermione* continues, as an homage to the fallen maestro. Half the Palace uproots itself. There is scarcely a carriage left in all of Paris, I imagine.

And by God, they love me when I descend from the heavens. Pallas Athene. A gift of wisdom in a day of what must seem like madness. A world without Lully? Unthinkable! And here he is, restored by music, Athena assuaging their fear, a balm against a mad world. That I receive their adoration is my gift to them, and they love me the more for it.

My newfound celebrity seems to have erased any scent of scandal that may have clung to the hem of my skirts. I have been invited to a ball. At the palace. Versailles. A return home in triumph, as a guest of Le Monsieur, the King's brother. This news in the form of a note, delivered backstage. I have caught someone's eye, it seems.

Should I go? Why do I hesitate? It is a stage I know well, although this character is new to them, the woman I have become.

Yes, I shall go. Oh, and to make such an entrance that they will all regret not having missed me more.

I have thought long about the woman I shall show them. The girl who ran away with her lover after a duel, the girl who slept in the woods, the tavern-singer on the road to Marseilles, the swordswoman, pistoleer, nun, seductress, arsonist, grave-robber, fugitive.

Diva.

When I am cold I have made the pleasant habit of draping d'Albert's crimson jacket about my shoulders. And it bears his scent still, despite these months apart.

So I send for a tailor, and have a cavalier's uniform made, down to the buttons, all of which are sourced from the same button-makers and licensed by the King. A wig, too, which cost something of a fortune. A man's wig.

And so attired, I make a convincing officer. There is to be no ball-gown for me. I dare not carry my pistol, in case someone recognizes its origin, or admires it overmuch and sends someone looking for its like in forgotten storerooms and armouries. But there is a sword by my side, and I practice the walk of those men whom I so admired on our travels from Tours. Confident. Deliberate. Bordering on haughty but neither delicate nor uncultured.

There is a fine black horse at the stables around the corner, and for a few sous he is mine for the evening. I have him fetched, and we set out across the bridge, south to the palace.

So much had changed.

Gone is the gravel approach, and the army of raking footmen. This is all paved now with bricks and black polished lamp-posts topped with gold leaf, making a colonnade of firelight. The sound of the horse's crisp echoing against the stone of buildings. This new road is a tendril reaching out to the city, and one day I swear Versailles will devour all of Paris itself.

But it is home, and my heart is light. In character as an officer, I must prevent myself from clapping at each familiar landmark. And here, too, I catch another flaw in my disguise: I laugh easily, but cannot force a man's laugh.

The hall itself is familiar—I am suddenly reminded of a bad fall down those very stairs as a young girl, and being frightened. But the cavalier, the man I am at this moment, is burdened by no such memory, and so I smile and take a glass from a tray, lifting the wine and saluting a gaggle of palace girls I do not recognize, all tittering behind their fans.

I will not lie and say my breast is devoid of ice. There is a sliver within, and it bears the name de La Reynie. I scan for him and his men, but faces change, and seeing none does not mean he is not here. I do not let the fear stop me. When do I?

The wine is a mistake. The girl, too, a mistake. But she is lovely.

There is a lotus pond, here, at the palace, with these mottled orange fish from China or Japan, I think. As long as your arm and gulping air. They appear to be made out of some kind of metal, not gold or copper but something in between. The boys around this woman remind me of those gulping fish, flashing in the sun, circling a perfect lotus in their center.

I catch Elise's eye across the floor, and while she does not recognize me at first, when she finally does she laughs and I try not to, lest my voice betray me.

She rushes over and kisses me, which is not scandalous in the slightest, as she kisses all the pretty boys and there I am, prettiest of all of them, so no surprises. She adores my disguise and assures me it is convincing but would be moreso were she on my arm.

She points out the latest pairings, liaisons, scandals and indiscretions. I suspect she would make the perfect spy, and the King should send her to some foreign court, though she would probably announce that she *was* a spy upon arriving, just to see the reactions. Still, were anyone willing to be hanged for a good story, it would be Elise.

And more wine. I cringe to admit it. Of course there would be no Champagne at such an event, only the stronger, headier grapes of my childhood. Regardless, the wine seems to vanish as fast as it appears. The heat of my jacket, the air devoured by a thousand, thousand candles, and I thirst and slake on endless wine.

And then I am face-to-face with the Lotus.

I am uncertain as to whether I merely wish to show them how it is to be done, or of any other reason. We dance, and I think myself clever to dance with her in disguise, with Elise squealing with delight in the background. The gulping fish were put out, and when they attempt to cut in, I rebuff them silently. I wish I could say that I am somehow defending the honour of the lovely Lotus, but I think rather they are simply spoiling my game.

There is a rough hand on my shoulder, and a word I do not catch but the implications of which are clear enough.

Oh God, had I any sense at all I would laugh and doff my wig and tear open my chemise, as I had that night on the road to Marseilles. Bare my breasts and make fools of them all. But I am too proud, and too ill-tempered. And my head, aflame, is thick with wine already.

I say little, as I do not want my woman's voice to give away my disguise. I have a right to be that cavalier, at this moment, of that I was certain. And they brought dishonour to my regiment, which of course I do not have. I lead with my chin to the door, and far too shortly after, we are in a garden just off the courtyard, in full view of the Swiss Guard.

As the first is finding his feet and still feeling the balance of his sword, I thrust him clean through the chest, like a pistol shot, turning away before he falls to ground. I fully expect the other two to rush me, but they do not. Their guard is perfect, their form disciplined. And no Marechal to knock me to my senses and drag me away in shame.

I send a feint to the one on my right, to provoke a response, but none is forthcoming. I circle him to put him between the one on my left, to keep them in a line, but they are too good for that. Their eyes flash to one another; a wordless plan.

When the attack comes it is stronger and faster than I anticipate, and I parry awkwardly. He presses the attack, but I take a long step back, to re-establish measure. I go for the disarm, finally sensible enough to be afraid, I think, but he knows all the conventional attacks for this, and avoids them ably.

I create a void, and he does not take my bait. He is patient, and his friend is circling around beside me.

I leap a small volta, effectively switching opponents, and feint a half-jab, high, even while I am off-balance. He falls for it, his own guard obscuring his vision for a moment, and I reached under and around his blade to his heart. In and out, without resistance. Not so much as the nick of a rib. The look of utter surprise on his face that it was over so quickly. This leaves me with one, thus far superior, opponent.

He is not enraged by the death of his friends, as one might be expected to be. His composure is pure, a creature of distilled training. I can elicit no error in his parry or his riposte. My breath begins to run ragged, as I become tired from the first two encounters, and honestly anything longer than thirty seconds of inhabiting a single line between life and death is exhausting. I fear, for the first time, the possibility that an opponent's point might find my heart. My ridiculous, enormous, drunken and wounded heart.

It is no fault of his that his guard drops just close enough to his hip that his blade straightens to precisely the correct degree. I use a glissade, a sliding of the blade, which causes it to reverberate and give control of the point to the opponent. Inside his guard now, I open his throat.

Three dead men, in less than a minute. Likely good men, from good families, well trained.

A waste. Which is why, of course, it is illegal and why the Swiss Guard seizes me at that very moment, the butt end of a halberd into my stomach, with another taking out the back of my knees. I am on the ground, gasping for breath like a golden fish, my officer's wig falling to the stones and my woman's hair, short though it is, framing my face.

I expect death, at this moment, but I am too busy trying to breathe to care.

When the blackness finally falls from my vision, I look up to see the soulless, chilling countenance of Monsieur Gabriel Nicolas de La Reynie, Lieutenant General of the Police.

From a letter found in the Biblioteque Nationale attributed to Mme. Julie La Maupin.

la Bastille

A dream of the sisters, and the bells of the monastery. I am to attend to the horses—one is sick—and yet I must run to the choir, and I will sing to God and the horse will die.

Why did we have horses? Some were left by arriving girls (whatever fate befell the dapple I rode from Marseilles is a mystery), others gifted ignorantly, not thinking horses need feeding and exercise and attention that is not exactly in measure with convent life. Others are to exchange on Sundays when the priest arrives for Mass, on one horse and departing on another. Back in the dream I am singing but at the same time attending to the tack for the priest's horse, and the priest is Sérannes now, and he wants to kiss me, and all the while I think

The horse is going to die. And it is all my fault.

I wake to a summons.

Arriving via liveried boy, in whose colours I do not know. But that is the Palace—an hour could pass and all the colours change by the whim of the King.

I recall a certain persimmon that was as hideous as it was fleeting.

My maid has been sent for, to attend to me properly, that I might be freed of this prison, to return to my home and make myself presentable.

The King will decide if I live or die. As always, I suppose, but one is never quite as aware of it as in such a time as this.

I am weary. So weary. Sick and thin and drawn, I chafe under regret and sorrow. Sorrow I know well, but regret is a new flavour that is ashen on my tongue.

I must go. And no time to thank the boy for his small kindnesses.

The staff are all silent. Their eyes are wide, but they look to the floor as I enter. I have some air of death about me, whether that of the three courtiers I have killed or my own, I cannot tell. My maid stuffs herself in the opposite corner of the carriage home, having dressed me in the prison. The chill set in her at once, I can see it in her face and the stiffness of her movements.

My tongue is sharper than usual. Even though the stone walls of prison have brought out the nun within. There is much to be accomplished, and I cannot have them all simpering when there is much to attend to.

I should be ravenous, but I crave only simple food. I bathe, but the water is not as hot as I prefer it.

I need sleep. They are to wake me at dawn. It is possible that in the morning, I go from the King to the headsman's axe. That, I expect, is to be the performance of a lifetime. Such an intimate thing, one's death. I feared the fires to which I was condemned at Aix, and I fled the henchmen of de La Reynie. But this new possibility I do not fear, or if so, not too much. Perhaps because I will be home, and my blood will feed the roses of the gardens I knew as a girl.

A kind of good-night to the world, then. To my world.

I do so adore this pink. The same pink as the ribbon I wore around my throat the night I threw myself upon Louis' mercies.

Oh, and the King.

Presented by de La Reynie's men, who come for me at breakfast, and hand me to the Swiss Guard, who are kind enough to escort me to the chapel, confession, and communion. And from thence to His Majesty.

What does one observe? He is beyond all observation. The air is quicker around him, and timeless. I have known Him all my life. He is the Sun, and all light is merely His reflection. He has created a world that it be so, created every movement, or hesitation, each step taken upon such a world, each word spoken within it. A man who crushed all hesitation, all doubt and regret decades before I was born. And hence, no longer a man.

We know you, He says.

Indeed, Your Majesty, I reply. My voice a little song.

And you killed three men, here, in my home? In a duel? He says.

As you say, Your Majesty. Each syllable like a note on the harpsichord. One, then another; I do not know how many words I have in my life to speak, so I savour each one.

And you are aware, He says, that We have banished duelling from Our realm?

At the time, Your Majesty, I say, it hardly seemed to matter.

He laughs at this. No, he says. I suppose it rarely does.

Well, He says, let Us have a look at you, and He takes both my hands, and His eyes trace my body, and the tops of my breasts and the well of the throat, and my chin and the line of my jaw and the shape of my lips and my eyes, which look down demurely, although no part of me shies away from being seen so. I am being evaluated not as a person, but as a landscape. Some image of France itself, and the King Himself, the artist. He seems to approve and purses His lips slightly.

Three? He says.

Three, Your Majesty.

Mm, He says curtly.

Mens rea, He says.

Your Majesty?

The guilty mind. Latin, He says. I know this, of course.

He continues. When We intended that Our subjects not indulge in the frivolity of duelling, We did not conceive that women should participate in such an undertaking. Therefore We could not be said to have mens rea in allowing an incident to go unpunished. The law does not pertain to women, and We must respect the law, He says.

Of course, Your Majesty, I say.

Without the guilty mind, We trespass no law in pardoning you, he says. We must respect the law, He repeats.

Of course, Your Majesty, I say again.

He smiles a grandfatherly smile, and nods, and departs, a swath of servants bowing low in his path and wake.

I curtsy low and perfectly, my blood roaring in my ears. Barely enough to hear him. I can hold this pose, deferential, bowed, for hours.

You sing beautifully, He says, from down the hall.

I can hear them. Backstage. The cast a blur of welcome kisses and settled bets, laughter and horror and grim humour and sweet tea for my throat. An embrace from Marthe, and Fanchon. The curtain rises, even as they place another hundred pins to fasten my helmet in my hair, even though the makeup leadens my lashes and stings my eyes.

They know I am coming for them, and they are delirious for my arrival. Rumour and scandal and gossip sweetening their expectations, sharpening their appetites. My descent from the heavens. I am back from the dead, alive only by the graces of wit and voice and steel, and I am here, here, in the Academie Royale de Musique in the Chateau de Saint-Germain-en-Laye, for them, for the love of them, and I am Athena, Wisdom Herself who settles upon them, a Goddess from rope and rafter among them at last.

And they adore me. Oh, how they adore me!

And when they see me, there is only one player upon the stage, and only one name upon their lips.

La Maupin!

And in their applause are notes of caramel, and cinnamon, and the sweet, perfect finish of pink sugar.

——◖●◗——

Just as in Marseilles, the devil approaches as if expected. That, I see now, was a rehearsal. This is the performance, here in the Café Procope, the rue des Fossés-Saint-Germain-des-Prés. The same stride, the same movements with the chair, the same gesture for coffee as before, months and miles away.

Monsieur Lieutenant General, I say, without looking up from my cup. I watch the steam.

Marvelous, your performance the other night, he says.

I should not have suspected you as fond of the Opera, Monsieur, I answer.

Oh, I take my distractions, he says. But that is not the performance of which I speak.

Oh? and that is all he shall get from me. He is trying to throw me off balance.

At the palace, he says. The duel. Perfect.

I give him nothing.

Are you not curious, he adds, as to the identity of those whom you have killed?

Again, nothing.

No? Well, he says, as his coffee arrives, regardless. Some matters were seen to, in that exchange. Matters of…mutual benefit.

For this I shall grant him one further Oh?

Indeed, he says. And then he succinctly recounts a series of names, problematic individuals and their sons, lands and politics, and how one certain fallen young officer, catching a smallsword to the heart in a palace duel over a pretty girl, changes some other conspiracy or tangle of affairs. Elise would know, she has a talent for such things.

I've bored you, he says, hurt.

Somewhat, I reply.

Well then, let us simply assume that you had agreed to my schemes from the outset, and that the result would be the same.

Meaning? I made to look as burdened as possible by his presence.

Meaning the thing I would have you do is done. Meaning the King is watching you too closely for me to seek such an arrangement in future. Meaning, I suppose—and with this he raises his cup to me—adieu.

So.

He thinks he has had me after all. Because his world has resolved by happenstance. He sees himself as the architect of all things. Including me.

That he had a right to my fate, and is now graciously freeing me of such.

Absurd. I almost feel sorry for him.

Almost.

But this is his final scene, his exit, and I shall let him enjoy it as he applauds himself off the stage of my life.

To La Maupin, he says, toasting me, and mocking me I think only slightly.

I raise the pale blue porcelain of the cup, watch the cream swirl gently as I do so.

La Maupin, I answer, with my most subtle smile.

fin

"In truth the story of La Maupin is so laden with passages of excitement and interest that any writer on the subject has only to make an agreeable choice of episodes sufficiently dramatic to form a cohesive narrative. The real difficulty one would have to contend against would be to remove the sordidness, the reckless passion, the unscrupulousness, the criminal intent which lies behind such a character."

— Bram Stoker –Author of *Dracula*

IF YOU ENJOYED *LA MAUPIN*,
MAKE SURE YOU DON'T MISS
WINTER BY WINTER,
THE EPIC BEGINNING TO
THE SWORD GIRL SERIES

"There were once women in Denmark who dressed themselves to look like men and spent almost every minute cultivating soldiers' skills... They put toughness before allure, aimed at conflicts instead of kisses, tasted blood, not lips, sought the clash of arms rather than the arm's embrace, fitted to weapons hands which should have been weaving, desired not the couch but the kill."

– The Danish Histories of Saxo Grammaticus,
12th Century

I remember giants from the earliest of times, they who raised me long ago. Nine worlds I remember, the nine great realms hanging from the world-tree, all beneath the earth.

A tall ash-tree, Yggdrasil, sprinkled with the white waters, from which come all the dews of the valleys, stands evergreen above the Well of Urd.

And to this tree come three wise maidens from the pool beneath. One maiden is called Urd, the other Verdandi, and the third Skuld. Past and present and future, together they carved the runes, issued laws, and gave orleg—fate— to the children of men.

— PART I —

A swan. Whiter than the mist, though dappled with red and orange. That's the fire's light reflected in her feathers. She swims on, calmly.

It's still morning. Mist on the water, and the sun has yet to chase the chill from the air.

A barn, and a drying shack, I seem to remember. That's the light that paints the swan, paints the mist. That's the fire. The stench of fish, so, probably. I've never spent much time on this beach, not really. But this family's home is in flames, or at least I think it belongs to the woman whose screams stopped only moments before. Moments or hours, it's difficult to keep track. It's like I'm waking up, but of course I've been awake for hours.

Hours and hours.

The toe of my boot makes little boat-prints in the sand. The smoke from the shack stings my eyes, as the soot has stained the mouths of many here, black smears around lips and noses, flecked with spittle and blood.

The rowers pulled the staves from the goat pen and made a sort of cage for us, a meandering arc like half a ship open to the tide. There is nowhere to go – even if the three hundred of us were to run into the sea we'd be visible from all sides of the bay, and an easy target for stones or archers. And then there is the chill of the bay itself, of course. Mostly children and grandmothers left, and not so many of us strong for swimming.

We could turn and overrun the goat-pen. But they have thirty men ashore with shields and axes, some still blood-drunk from the night's work. Each of them could cleave a dozen of us before we reached the trees, and then they'd run out of people to kill.

Even if we made it, where to go? There are another hundred men sorting through what's left of the village. Little silver, if any, so that means grain and meat, some wire and iron. Nothing worth dying for. So even if I pushed past this small crowd, sick and lowing with grief, through the shore-hammered rank of posts, and somehow made it through the men who reek of smoke, and sweat, and blood, when they stand close and if some weapon found my hand, how many of them could I kill before the trees and then? And then? Then home, in flames or perhaps just ash and smoke now, it's been hours, and only more killing, them or me or both. But I don't move.

I hold my sisters close. Kara, exhausted, has stopped crying. Her fingers seem tiny when she reaches out to play with my hair, not as blonde as hers, but still blonde as ashwood. Rota hasn't cried, but she's shaking with anger. Rota would have killed three or four of these rowers before dying, I think, but she stays with us, to protect us. That's her.

We were taught, all of us, to pray in such hours. To swear vengeance or keen for those who now trudge whatever road to the doors of Valhalla. But I see little of this. We're still too bruised, too numb.

I'm thirsty.

We shuffle away from the rising tide, flotsam pushing us against the staves. It makes the men nervous, and their grip chokes up on their axe handles in anticipation. But we aren't going to do anything. They won't kill us all.

The biggest treasure is not whatever they might find in the village—not the bronze bell, or the plows, and tools, or scant silver. It is ourselves. Those of us who survive the journey will do well at the slave-markets of Upsalla, or Birka.

It can't be the cruelest of lives, to be in thrall. You rise, you work, you feed, you sleep. I've never seen a slave mistreated. They're too expensive. There is no freedom, no, not for yourself or any children you might have. But that's not so different to village life. And everything can be taken from you, just as it has from me, in the hours before dawn. They'll make me a slave then.

But it would kill me to be separated from my sisters, so I think we would all rather die.

I'm not myself. I am not the temper every villager knew and feared since I could walk. I am a numb thing, a frozen thing, cowed and broken.

I'm looking at myself, scared and tangled and matted, the drying blood of others on my dress and my face, and somehow I'm laughing. Just laughing. I can't stop.

Kara's eyes are wide. She's frightened of my laughter. But the thought of me as a slave is too ridiculous, and it's outweighing my self-pity.

Me, Ladda, a slave. I can't imagine it. Nor could anyone else. I used to bite people when I was small just for asking me to do anything, let alone ordering me around.

So I'm laughing and Kara shushes me. She's afraid, afraid that the men will come closer or take me from her or notice me at a time she desperately, so desperately, wishes to be invisible.

"You!" he says, one of the rowers who has penned us, herded us against the ice of the tide. "You'll laugh through a hole in your throat if you can't shut your mouth."

"I already have more than one hole to laugh at you with," I snort. The folk around me cringe as though bitten. The rower comes closer.

"I'll fill your holes with my axe," he says. It's a game now, but he doesn't know it.

"I think your axe is too small to fill any hole," I say, and the older women snicker despite themselves.

"Come here," he commands. I laugh again, though by now Rota has put her thick arms around Kara and drawn her backwards into the crowd of aunts and grandfathers.

"This is my beach," I tell him. "My land. Mine. You don't command me. You're no Jarl, and no husband, and no mother." I don't move. Honestly, I have nothing to lose by taunting him.

Nothing but my life.

"If you come closer, I will drown you in this very bay," I say, which is either challenge or invitation.

He doesn't know what to do.

"Look. That was an offer," I say. "You come over here and I'll drown you, and you can go bathed to your gods. It might take some time to get the fish stink out of you..."

"Bitch!" he barks. This just makes me laugh louder, and others are joining in. It's crazy. I'm getting us all killed. What in the name of Hel am I doing?

"That is a thing boys say to women when they are afraid," I say. "Don't be afraid, little boy. Come here and let me bathe you. Or are you going to threaten me with your... little... axe?" I illustrate this insult by lifting my little finger and wiggling it in the cool salt air. The aunts all laugh out loud now.

Enraged, he turns himself sideways to wriggle through a space in the posts, but he snags himself on his belt. I dip to the shore and take a handful of sand in one and a rock in the other.

He's free now and five, four, three paces from me, so I throw the sand into his eyes and the rock to his forehead. One of the aunts sticks out a foot, and he's on his knees on the beach.

I step back because I don't need to see what's happening to him, as the lame uncles and little boys, the aunts and grandmothers of the village, all grab whatever they can of the man and pull, pull hard, until he is torn open by their fury and their retribution, until he's a picture of the wounds we all bear now, drawn in flesh and spray and jutting bone.

Some of us have started to die. The other rowers have seen this havoc and have thrown axes and stabbed spears into the pen. Some are stupid enough to join their comrade, though those are soon dragged to their deaths, even though five, eight, a dozen of ours die to one of theirs. Each stone thrown from the pen is a spear tip thrust into it, until we settle and drag our dead closer to the water, though we can't say why. We have been, for a brief moment, agents of our own death, and that is enough of a life for some.

I would pray to Skathi, or Vor as my mother would want me to do. But it is still not the time for prayer.

One of theirs jerks like a puppet. Mouth thrown open, hands wide, head snapped back. A story-teller conveying surprise, though awkwardly. Comically. And his companion too: jerked back, shoulder-bitten.

Maybe someone in the pen has been praying. Maybe I should have been doing the same.

Then a third rower struck, though in falling we see the arrows jutting out of him, and the rowers turn and scan the beach.

I don't remember picking up this axe. It's curious. I remember my first comb, the first fish I ever speared. I remember deciding to run away from home when I was very small, planning the night before what bread I should take with me and a small pot of honey. I remember the face of the first drowned man I ever found, and the second. But how the axe came to my hand I can't say, and if you told me the goddess herself had put it there, I couldn't argue with you.

It's a small axe, the head the width of my palm, the handle alder. A throwing axe.

So I throw it and it finds the back of the skull of one of the Swedish rowers, the shock of his death reverberating through the air and back into my hand like I never let go.

The rowers turn now and run to the tree line above the beach. I'm stupid for a moment and simply stand there thinking about the man I've just killed. Two men, I suppose. One with my tongue, the other with that axe. I walk forward slowly to retrieve it when I see the posts are gone, trampled into sand, and the villagers tear after the fleeing men before they can escape.

More are coming. More men. A ship's worth of shields, maybe two. Yes, a full crew of eighty men and women, and whatever sunlight makes it through the mist glances off spear tips and axes and even a sword.

I think they've come to cut us down.

But among the men there are archers, and they let loose a volley into the backs of the retreating rowers. None make it to the forest, each with a thigh- or a shoulder-full of shaft and fletching and screams.

As the last of them falls, the eighty descend on them in a roar. Shields are driven into spines and skulls of our captors. The beach is a crunch and a howling.

Something moves past me, solid and fast as a boar. Though it misses me, the air around it shakes, slammed like a door. The fallen man, his back in the sand and now without his spear, looks at me with panic.

"Kill me," I say.

He looks for his friends dying on the beach, and back to me, not understanding.

"Well?" I challenge. "You have arrows in your leg. Pull one of them out and kill me with it."

He almost does it. He grips a shaft and winces, but that's all I need, and I fall on him, both hands on the axe handle, with all my weight, all my fifteen years of village life uprooted and lifted and hurled to the earth on the blade of an axe-head, crushing sternum and ribs and heart and ribs again.

The studs of his leather shirt bite through my dress into my knees. It hurts. My throat hurts, too, from thirst I think, but no, it's because I've been screaming, roaring, growling into the face of this dead man, this corpse whose shirt is hurting my knees through my dress, which I'll have to wash in the sea, or dye, because I've emptied him of blood and it clings to the wool and how long has this howl been in my throat?

Rota's arm wraps around my waist and lifts me up like I'm a doll. Even though she's fourteen, a year younger, she's stronger than me, stronger than anyone. There's an axe over her shoulder, sticky with blood.

"Come, sister," she says. "Ladda, come on."

I nod, looking back towards the water, catching a glimpse, over Rota's shoulder, of a single white swan.

"Take me to their camp," I ask Rota, still outside myself. The ones who killed the rowers, I mean.

"They're not setting camp," she answers. "They're going to follow them North, to Nidaros in the Trondelag."

"How do you know?" My voice is still hoarse, and I'm combing blood and sand out of my hair with my fingers.

"I heard them talking," she says. "Made sense to listen."

I nod. "I should go back. To the village."

"No," Rota answers again. "There's nothing." And she places in my palm a disk in silver, cold and hard, folding my fingers over it. A brooch. Our mother's. I can tell without looking. I search her eyes.

She shakes her head. The slightest of movements. So.

"Where's their chieftain?" How long was I on the beach? I look to the trees for shadows, but the fog has barely lifted and there's no telling the hour. A day without hours. Fitting.

Rota nods a direction, and I stumble following her. I take her hand, and it's only then I see she's cut her hair. Ragged, the line. Hurriedly, with a knife. Her hair is sometimes brown, sometimes copper in the light. I would braid it for hours when we were young, but I've stopped years ago. There are only Kara's birch-white locks to braid now.

"Kara," I say, remembering.

"She's... alright," Rota says. "She's safe. Come on. We should hurry, they're getting ready to leave."

Three men, in a circle of men. One tall and broad, with a youth's scruff of beard on the end of his chin like a goat, his hair pulled back in a knot. He stands easy, like he's waiting for fish or peeling an apple. Like war was nothing.

The other older, but not by much, and clearly wealthy by his tunic and collar. The third an advisor, with sun-bronzed skin and kind eyes, a step behind his wealthy master. The men around them part to make room for us, Rota and me.

"I killed a wolf once," calls out the bearded youth to me. "It was watching a squirrel up a tree. So I speared the wolf. Today, you were our squirrel."

"You were watching?" I ask.

"Waiting," he says. "We've been following these ships for three days. They must have thought us farther behind..."

"I'm no squirrel," I tell him.

The bronze-skinned advisor steps forward, smiling faintly. His eyes are brown. "This is your King, Ragnar, King of the Vestfold and of Jutland."

I pause. He doesn't look like a king. He is very tall, but his clothes are rough, and his breeches are unshorn goatskin so the sand and salt cling to the hairs lashed to his legs with leather thong. He looks half-animal at best.

"King," I say.

I reach up towards him and slap his face as hard as I can, my mother's brooch digging into my palm in my other hand as it makes an involuntary fist. There is a roar of laughter, as Ragnar dramatically staggers, rubbing his face for comic effect, mocking me. I have every right to expect a spear in my ribs now, but I don't care.

"King?" I yell. "You bring war to my village and I'm supposed to welcome you like a king? Where were you at dawn? We're all dead, save for the grandmothers and children! Some king." I spit at his feet. My hand hurts.

He considers this. He looks to one of his men and points, accepts something from him.

"For you, then, not-a-squirrel. Take it."

He hands me a sword without a scabbard. I take it, and it's lighter than I expect it to be. There are runes set into the blade, but I can't make them out,. I'm too exhausted and too angry and too thirsty to read.

"I can't feed my people with this," I tell him.

"That's no ordinary blade," he says carefully. "It's worth the price of a kingdom."

I thrust the sword's handle back toward him. "So sell me one."

He doesn't accept it, but he smiles, and not unkindly.

"You can't stay here," Ragnar says. "They may wheel back to escape us, or Fro may send for more ships."

"Fro?" I've never heard the name.

"King of Uppsala," says the counsellor. "His armies have killed your people and your king, Sivard. Ragnar has come to avenge him." I haven't heard any of this. Not a rumour.

"Do you have somewhere to go?" asks Ragnar. "Kaupang?"

"Kaupang?" I ask. "We are farmers. Fishers. We have no business in Kaupang. There's barely three hundred of us left. The market would swallow us whole."

"You would be safe," he replies.

"We wouldn't be anything," I answer. "No stories. No village. No names. We'd be undone."

"Somewhere else, then," says Ragnar's companion, the rich one. "Somewhere safe. Together."

"This man," says the advisor, "is Jarl Rorik, from Aalborg."

"A Jutlander," I say.

He nods. "Give me your name," he says. His voice is soft, the only softness I've seen in a lifetime, this new lifetime that began in the night.

"Hladgertha." I give him my proper name.

"I am sorry, Hladgertha," says the Jarl, "for what has happened to your people. And I would shelter them if I could. But Ragnar is right. It's not safe for you to remain here. You could go inland, or well north—but even then, the coast is not safe until Fro is dead."

"His head will hang from my boat," says Ragnar. But I've heard this before, men puffed up with the talk of war. All the boys with scruff-beards spoke like this all the time, until their lives were cut from them in the night. I try not to think of their bodies smouldering and cooling in the air, not a hundred famnr from this place.

"What boat?" I ask.

"We have a dozen skeid," Ragnar tells me. "You know boats?"

"My father... our father, is... was... a boatbuilder. Knarr, mostly. We sold them." I'm a thousand years old on this beach, I'm thinking. Remembering that other life, the life from last night, presses me into the sand.

"Do not set out in boats," warns Rorik. "Even if you have them." Which we don't—the rowers took everything seaworthy, towing them or setting them on fire—so it's a warning wasted.

"The Gaular," says Rota. "Our uncle has a lodge in the Gaular valley." I look at her, remembering. Summer's end, years ago. A journey, but not a deadly one. A run of salmon and my uncle's hall. A waterfall and a green forest soft with moss.

My uncle is here among the ashes of the dead. I don't think he'll mind.

Rorik looks to me. "The Gaular, then," he says.

I nod, thinking. "It will take a day for us to round up the goats. Some sheep, cattle, whatever's left."

"In the morning, then," says Rorik. "But do not mourn your dead until you are safe. Tonight, they drink from Odinn's own cup." These are meant to be kind words, but they fall to the beach before they can reach me.

Again, I nod. I thank Skathi for Rota's strength when I realize my hand has been on her shoulder, steadying myself, my other hand clutching both the brooch and the sword handle.

I turn, forgetting the king for a moment, and turn back to him. Ragnar.

"Your breeches," I begin. "Why would a king from the Jutland wear goatskin?"

It's an odd question, but he laughs. A story he's used to telling. "To keep adders away," he says.

"But," I reply, "we don't have adders in this part of the Nordvegr."

His blue eyes sparkle. "Then the breeches must be working."

Brushing Kara's hair calms us both—maybe she's too calm. In shock. Far off, as though she sailed away from the slave-pen on the beach, and the tide has yet to bring her back. She's clean, impossibly clean in her yellow dress with the blue apron, large oval brooches in copper like the unblinking eyes of some weird creature.

We haven't put up a shelter, as the sun has warmed these stones a little, and the moss is soft. Rota approaches, solid, and strong. She's changed out of her dress and into breeches, and found a rust-coloured woolen cloak from somewhere. I force myself to not scan the thing for blood stains.

Rota brings us steaming broth in a bowl for sharing. I thank her for this, but Kara says nothing.

"Do we have a number?" I ask Rota. She's been on task, and I doubt a drop of this soup has touched her lips.

"Two hundred seventy," she tells me. "No one alive between sixteen and fifty."

I nod. What else is there to do? We're now two tribes divided by a lifetime, the too young and the too old.

"The men have called a Thing," she tells me. "Sunset."

"Sunset is too late," I say. "Decisions need to be made now."

"You need to address them, Ladda," Rota says. "Tell them what the king told you."

"Why would they listen to me?"

"They're saying the gods have chosen you. When you lured that rower to his death." She sounds excited about this, and it should sicken me. But it doesn't.

"I got so many of us killed," I say. "It was reckless."

"We were all dead anyway. Dead or in thrall, all of us. We'd be in iron collars now if not for you." She sees my discomfort at this. "It's what they're whispering," she says, "and I know it's true."

Kara's voice is small. "It is my fault," she says. I hand her the wooden bowl which she takes with numb fingers.

"How? Shush now," I tell her. "You didn't bring Fro's men to us. Ragnar did that. Or some working of war, anyway. Jarls and kings. But not you."

"I dreamt it. All of it," she says, as though reciting something. Stumbling to remember. "The killing. The dying. The pen. The beach." Finally, she looks at me, after hours of dreamlike distance. "You."

"Just a dream," I say.

Rota speaks up. "If the gods give you a dream, they should tell you what to do with it," she tells our little sister. "It's their fault."

"I should have said," she answers.

"And we would have done what?" I ask, trying to hide my frustration. "Post guards? Uproot the village? It's already on us, and no one is guarding. No one is even packing." I play with a string of dry grass, tying a knot to make a wish, though I forget to before the knot is complete. I let it fall.

"Some of the boys have gone to get the goats, bring the sheep in," says Rota. And yes, if we listen, we can hear the bleat of them getting closer, though we can't see them from where we sit. We can see smoke, though, and don't speak of it.

There's movement behind the stones to the south. For all of us, our hearts hammer blood into our fingers, our faces suddenly cold. An indrawn breath of panic, shared between the three of us.

Comically, a long snout emerges, grey and with loose tufts of fur, and a black button of a nose. A great elkhound, with no small amount of wolf in his ancestry, looking for its master.

"He's dead, shaggy one," I call out. "They're all dead. Seek your master in Valhalla."

His eyes seem to understand.

"I'm sorry," says Kara quietly, holding out her palm.

Tamely, the dog trots towards us, three sisters in the pale sun.

ABOUT THE AUTHOR

Jordan Stratford has been pronounced clinically dead, and was briefly (mistakenly) wanted by INTERPOL for international industrial espionage. He has won numerous sword fights, jaywalked the streets of Paris, San Francisco, and São Paulo, and was once shot by a stray rubber bullet in a London riot. He lives in the crumbling colonial capital of a windswept Pacific island, populated predominantly by octogenarians and carnivorous gulls.

He has been featured on *c/net, io9, boingboing, WIRED,* and *Reading Rainbow* and is represented by Silvia Molteni at Peters, Fraser + Dunlop in London.